# FREDONIA BOUND
## By
## SannaBlue Baker

### BURIED WHERE WE STAND
When God handed down judgement with a Winchester rifle… the historical secret of a community in post Civil War Georgia. A secret still kept today.

### THE HEALING STREAM
A hidden mountain stream plays a role in healing an injured traveler. The story is revealed of miracles, feuds and saving loved ones.

### FIVER DEAN
As one of the world's most wanted art thieves, if Fiver Dean can survive the attack by the Albatross, he might escape Interpol and a vindictive female Agent.

This is a work of fiction. Names, characters, places and incidents are either the product of the author's imagination or used fictitiously, and any resemblance to actual persons living or dead, business establishments, events , or locales, is entirely coincidental.

**Fredonia Bound**
COPYRIGHT ©2023 by Gary 'SannaBlue' Baker

All rights reserved. No part of this book may be used or reproduced in any manner whatsoever without written permission of the author, except in the case of brief quotations embodied in critical articles or reviews.
Contact Information – sannablue@icloud.com

Publishing History
First Edition, 2023

**Dedicated
To My Son
Gareth 'G-Man' Wesley Baker**

# buried where we stand

## When God handed down Judgement
### with a Winchester rifle...

# Buried Where We Stand

## Chapter One
## Pain Keeps Memories Alive

The Reverend Josiah Tallman stood by the cracked, church window of the historic landmark, and looked outside. He squinted his eyes to make out where the parishioners were gathering around the tables on the ground. He relished his time in the old church building, because he only came here one day a year now, to meditate and pray. He put his large hand against the window frame and shifted his weight off his bad, right knee.

Outside was a flurry of activity. The ladies on the 'Tallman Day Celebration' Committee, were instructing several of the menfolk where they wanted each table placed in an area beneath the huge oak tree. Other ladies, of the church, were taking white tablecloths and covering each table, once it was in the right position.

Scores of church members were coming down a path, leading from the entrance of the church property, back to the tables where the dining area was being assembled. Each person, walking, was carrying different sizes of cardboard boxes, packed full, of a different assortment of covered meats, vegetables and desserts. The air was pungent with the kitchen offerings of fried corn, sweet potatoes, and every kind of bean and green, you could imagine. Platters of buttered, mash potatoes lay
 dormant, waiting to be drowned in layers of brown gravy. This was the biggest dinner on the grounds the church had every year. The event was to honor the anniversary of The Reverend Josiah Tallman, arriving at the tiny meeting house many years ago. In later years, the small

congregation would grow and become one of the largest and most active, churches in the county.

Reverend Tallman had arrived at the little Georgia church when he was a young man of thirty years old. The old church was originally started in 1868, in a little remote community in Georgia. The secluded and somewhat desolate area, where former slaves had settled, was so far from any established town, it wasn't even on any map of the state. An enterprising citizen, started a General Store, and eventually, a post office was established at the store... and being how the General Store's owner's name was John Johnson, they named the little city, Johnsonville.

For many years, the godly Reverend, had been honored yearly for his service and sacrifice to the Ebenezer African Methodist Church, with a spectacular day of celebration consisting of the dinner on the ground, and a special evening service with a guest speaker...but most of all, there was the music. The Ebenezer African Methodist Church Choir would go all out in the Sunday morning service, with praise songs that would literally rattle the roof of the new sanctuary. It was a most glorious service every year, and the church was always packed.

Reverend Tallman positioned his weight by the window. He slid his hand across the wall, and his fingers stopped in series of round holes that went all the way through the wall. He looked higher into the darkness of the upper roof of the historic building.

Streams of light. Up and down. Holes in the wall. A lot of holes.

Bullet holes.

The sound of children, playing on a swing set across from the dinner area, drifted through the hewn log planks of the old building. Pastor Tallman, smiled and gave praise to the Lord on how the church had been blessed by an abundance of kids and young people. That's the only way a church survives, he thought… children. God's gift. The preacher was alway sadden when he thought of what he had missed out by not marrying, and having children of his own. Just wasn't in God's plan, he guessed.

He marveled at the number of white people working out in the yard. They were committed members of the church congregation. I've seen a lot of God's miracles, he thought. Good, hard working people of different colors, working for the betterment of their surroundings and spreading the word. Praise God, he thought.

He took a step closer to the window, and raised his arm higher to a blackened area in the top corner of the window casing.

The burnt wood had weakened with the years.

The old preacher debated when he should go out and bless the food. The pastor's appearance was alway the official green light, to get the feed bag on, find a place in line, and fix yourself a plate. It was a time to enjoy the food, the music, and the companionship of family, good friends and neighbors. Dinner on the grounds! Good God Almighty and Praise the Lord! If you've never been to one, you have missed out. They used the dinner as an opportunity to raise funds for various mission charities, the church operated in Haiti and African nations. Churches from different denominations, and business people from all over the county, would bless the church with large contributions. All the money went to fund the missions, in Reverend Tallman's name.

They're not quite ready, the Reverend thought, as he watched more boxes being brought down the path by another group of people arriving at the event. The preacher had not seen a crowd like this in some time. There were people from not only across the county , but across the state. He felt humbled and unworthy to be fussed over with such a tremendous affair. To God be the glory, he thought to himself.

He moved over another window and to the church pew where he normally stayed, when he was in the old building, and sat down. He could see the current church building and the magnificent steeple, the church members had constructed,. The second building had gotten so small, for the growing congregation, the members constructed a much larger and beautiful sanctuary on a different part of the property. The original building had not been used for a long time. The original church building was originally built in 1868. Due to the historical significance, several church members had petitioned the government for recognition. They were successful and the one room, church was recognized on the National Register of Historic Sites. It was protected. Nobody was ever going to demolish this old building, thought the old pastor.

He had knelt in front on that old church pew, in the past, and prayed for his flock's salvation on many occasion. In the wobbly pulpit on Sunday mornings, he would left his head to heaven and pull God down to earth in an elegant and articulate prayer. The old church members would pass on to heaven through the years, and leave the church and their memory to their children and grandchildren. The grandchildren, maybe even great-grandchildren, the old preacher had baptized as babies in the creek behind the church, were now adults with children of their own.

The preacher felt tired and old as he watched through the window at some little boys, chasing some dogs that had gotten a whiff of the food.

He moved his head slightly out of a stream of bright sunlight, coming through the bullet holes in the wall. It was blinding his view of all the movement going on outside.

He vividly remembered those holes. The memory of how they got there was burned into his mind.

He closed his eyes and thought how had it not been for the grace of God, this old church and the huge sanctuary, with the newly paved parking lot, would not be here.

He closed his eyes, and in his darkness tried to stop the sounds from that night long ago.

He pushed on his temple with a large index finger, trying to muffle the sounds in his head.

The sound of the dogs.

The hiss of the fire.

And the sounds of prayers to God Almighty.

The large man bowed his head, stirred to tears from the memory.

In the midst of his emotion from the memory, the sound of dogs, howling in the distance, filtered through his senses and he was startled into alertness. He opened his eyes to discover the sky had darkened and it was like nighttime .

It wasn't the sound of the dogs that startled the old preacher, or the disappearance of the sun.

It was the sound of someone banging on the front door of the church.

Someone was screaming to be let in.

---

## Chapter Two - A Preacher Bleeds Like Any Man

Von Lucas rounded the corner of the road with his heart singing to the heavens. The moon shadows that followed his path down the dark, dirt road, seem to dance in jubilation with each stop he took.

She had said yes. She had really said yes.

The girl he had been chasing, for going on three years, had finally agreed to marry him.

He started humming and thinking of what all he would do, in welcoming his new bride.

It was dark, traveling down the narrow road, but the three quarter moon gave off enough light to see where he was going without a lantern or a torch. Besides that, it didn't matter if he stumbled on a rock or two in the middle of the road… he felt like he was walking on air.

He was traveling to his home on Nelson's Ridge. He had left from Mary's cabin, in Houston's Hollow, where she lived with her Papa, Momma and her Grand-momma. Several of the Houston boys, who were notorious bullies and of a violent nature, had been trying to court Mary Green also, and had threatened Von's life if they caught him messing around their territory. Mary did not want Von in any kind of fight, so Von had avoided the problem by calling on her late at night, when most people would be in bed. He had snatched the most beautiful girl in the county right from under their noses.

His chest was full of happiness and he skipped a few steps to hurry through the darkness.

As he rounded the bend in the road, from behind a large tree, a dark shape suddenly appeared and hurled through the air directly at Von.

Aaaaarrrraaa, the creature yelled, jumping, with an upraised arm and one hand in an attack position.

Whatever it was, landed right in front of the startled Von.

Von stopped in his tracks. Scared.

He didn't move. Too late to run.

He froze.

A man's face, with a huge grin, appeared through the dim light, as laughter cut the night's stillness.

'Got ya," the intruder said. He was standing not more than two feet away from Von.

All thoughts of wedding plans had disappeared from Von's mind.

Instead a wave of anger flowed through his arm to his hand, causing the hand to become a fist, causing the fist to land on the intruder's jaw with such an impact, it put the laughing man on his backside in the middle of the dirt road.

"Theo, boy, are you crazy?' Von whispered loudly to the his fallen, and now quiet, friend, he had just knocked down, "Don't you be jumping at me in the dark!"

Theo Cooker picked himself up slowly and rubbed his chin. He was enjoying his prank to much to feel any pain.

"I was just joking with you, Mr. Von, sir. I heard you coming a half mile down the road. I knew you were calling on Miss Mary Green tonight… and don't tell me to be quiet. You were humming loud enough somebody with a gun think you be a Midnight Canary. You got to admit though. It was funny…Did you pee yourself? Tell me, I scared you didn't I?

Theo started laughing again. He dusted his clothes off and reached over to pick up a large sack he had dropped, when Von hit him.

"Yea, you scared me," said Von, turning to continue

to walk down the road, " I was getting ready to put a blade into you. What you got in the bag?"

Theo hoisted the bag over his shoulder and fell in beside him.

"Oh just some chickens that ran off. Mama told me not to come home until I found them."

Von glanced over at him in the darkness. He didn't need the light of day to know a lie when he heard one.

"Those chickens sure must have been unhappy living with you, cause they've done ran five miles to find another home," he said, "how come they ain't cackling with joy, now that you've found them."

"Funny thing about that," Theo said, struggling to keep up with the taller man, "they were so excited to see me, their hearts gave out on them and they fainted right in front of me. I tied up them up with twine to make them feel safe, until I get them back on familiar ground"

"Theo," Von said, chiding the midnight chicken rustler, "you're going to be hanging from a tree one day."

"Yea, maybe so," said Theo, unrepentant," but, my last meal will be fried chicken."

Chicken and pig stealing were considered a serious offense in Stuart County. It was interesting Von thought, most of the people who thought it was a serious offense, were the people who owned the chickens and pigs. Other folks, less fortunate and with hungry mouths to feed, were more inclined to not pass up a chicken or pig that got loose after someone unlocked the pen. It just seemed like the right thing to do.

Recently, night patrols had been formed by some of the wealthier farmers to try and keep the thefts to a minimum. Anybody caught stealing, by these patrols, were dealt with harshly. Anything from a whipping to a hanging, was considered appropriate punishment. But, there was a lot of country to patrol, and the nightriders couldn't be everywhere at once.

Von laughed at his friend. He didn't want too. He couldn't help himself.

"Come on, let's move. I've got an early day tomorrow." He sped up his pace on the moonlit road.

"Slow down there some, high pockets,' Theo said, 'I want to get there the same time as you….Wait what it that?'

The two men suddenly stopped.

A faint howl had drifted up through the darkness. It had an eerie echo that forced a cold chill to run up the back of both men.

Von let a long breath of air out. He knew that sound. It was the sound nobody of color wanted to hear. Especially at night.

"Dogs. They've put the dogs on you!"

Theo started a faster pace of walking.

"No, couldn't be. I was careful," he said, "old man Winston was dead asleep. Nobody was stirring."

"Oh no," Von said, "not old man, Winston. You mean to tell me you stole chickens from the richest white man in these parts. Are you crazy or want to die at an early age?"

The sound of the dogs got louder and more distinct in the fact there was a large number of animals in the pack. Von started a slow run. Four miles. It was four miles home.

"All right, Theo, we've got to get out of here. We can't get caught out in the dark, Not if you have been thieving chickens."

Theo started running with Von. The sack of chickens bounced off his back with each step.

The dogs sounded closer and were obviously moving at a fast pace. As they ran down the road, Von turned his head toward Theo and motioned toward the sack on his back.

"Not too sure if we get caught you want them chickens on you," he said, in between breaths.

"Yea," Theo said, " you be right." Reaching back into the sack he pulled out a bird , freed it from the twine, and released it into the trees along the road. After running another twenty yards, he reached in, got another bird and did the same thing. He did this five times. After the last bird, he threw the sack high into the trees. It was too dark to see where it landed.

"Maybe, it will slow those devil dogs down a bit," he gasped. He had been having trouble keeping up with Von with the extra weight.

Von shook his head. "Five chickens? You stole five chickens? Lord help."

They broke into a steady run down the road, toward safety and home.

Within ten minutes of running, both of the young men could tell they were not going to out run the dogs. The incessant howling had picked up in tempo and loudness as the pack of dogs followed the chosen scent. They were moving fast. Mixed in with the sound of the dogs was the accompaniment of horse hoofs, adding to the sense of desperation of the running men.

"We ain't going to make it," Theo gasped as they ran, "what we going to do? We can't out run them."

The two ran further down the road, the once jubilant moonlight shadows, now had a sinister nature, as they ran through the darkness on the narrow road. They suddenly came upon a break in the trees and a downward slope in the terrain.

"Come on, " Von said, impulsively pulling on Theo's shirt, the two men ran off the road and down into the break among the trees, "I know what we can do. Preacher will help. We can cut over Black Oak Creek. He'll hide us, or know what to do. Come on, faster."

In the darkness and off the cleared road, they found the path that led down to the creek. Stumbling over rocks and small bushes, they entered the shallow creek and ran upstream until they came to a large pool of water where the church held it's baptisms. It became too deep to wade. Climbing a ravine that surrounded the pool, they emerged from the woods to a clearing where the church stood. They hesitated, trying to catch their breath.

The loud howls of the dogs behind them reached a higher pitch. The fastest dogs were already at the creek. The two men could hear the whines as the trackers milled around, searching where the scent had disappeared. It was only a matter of time, and time was running out.

"Come on, let's go," Von said, starting to run toward the front door of the church.

The church folks had built a small room, on the back of the building, to serve as a parsonage for their new pastor. Accustom to sleeping out in the elements for three years of the war, the new minister was enjoying the comfort of the small room, with an inside water hand pump, a pot belly stove, a rope bed covered by an old army blanket, and a pillow, made of an old flannel, shirt stuffed with straw. The extravagance of having four walls, made the him feel guilty sometimes, for living in so much comfort.

The dirt floor beside the bed, was packed down as hard as a brick. It where Reverend Tallman spent a goodly portion of his time, on his knees. A talk with the Lord, always started and ended his days. There was a rectangular cedar chest, at the foot of the bed, that doubled as a table. The reverend had been tossing and turning on his rope bed ever since he had laid down. The faint sound of hounds in the darkness, kept him from totally relaxing and letting sleep take over. It was now way past midnight, headed toward sunrise.

A sudden and violent knocking on the church's front door, brought him fully awake. Accustomed to moving quickly at a moment's notice or to the sound of a bugle, he lurched out of bed and grabbed for his pants and shirt. Dressing hurriedly, he reached over, opened the cedar chest and took out a revolver. Lighting a coal oil lamp, he checked the load of the gun and then ran out the room and into the sanctuary of the church.

"All right, All right," he yelled as he stumbled, carrying the lamp to the front door and flinging it open.

Von Lucas stood in light of the coal oil lamp, in front of the door of the church, pleading, "Help us, Preacher," he said. He was breathing hard, holding on to the door sill for support. "It's going to be trouble if they catch us, " he continued, "you got to help us!"

Through gasps of breath from the exhausted man, the preacher learned of the chicken theft and the men's attempt to get home. Reverend Tallman knew of the hired night riders, who were searching the roads, for chicken or hog thieves. Mr. Winston had probably hired them to protect his property.

Theo stood behind Von, leaning on the church steps. He was bent over, breathing heavily. "It was me, preacher, I was the one who done it, " he said, "Von didn't have anything to do with it."

The sound of the hounds was becoming more excited as the scent they were following became stronger.

"Come on in, boys, hurry up now" the preacher said, holding the door of the church open for them, " Come on in God's house."

The two exhausted runners followed the large minister to the back of the church, and through the doorway to his room. He motioned to the pump and a metal cup. The two men eagerly pumped water into the cup, and took turns gulping it down.

Reverend Tallman opened the cedar chest, and took out a double barrel Remington 10 gauge shotgun and a Winchester lever action rifle. The man of God was no stranger to fighting in his past life. He thought that was all behind him. He wanted only to love his fellow man. He kept weapons after the war…just in case any of his fellow man didn't want to love him back.

The preacher grabbed his hat and threw the weapons over his shoulder.

"Quick, now, " he said hurriedly to the younger men and pointed to the window of the back room, 'get yourself back through the meadow back of the church, and keep going north of the creek. Head up stream until you get to Samuel Waters, tell him to hide you out. Go on boys, don't look back. I'll take care of these fellows.

"What about the dogs?" Theo said, tensed to run.

"Here, give me your shirt."

Theo took off his shirt, flung it toward the preacher.

Von hesitated. "No, I won't leave you preacher," he said, "I ain't running no more. I'm staying here. I didn't do anything wrong. His determined tone dissuaded any argument from the pastor. "Go ahead,' Von continued, motioning to Theo, "Stay low and off the ridges. You'll make it."

Theo pushed opened the thin paned window. He slung one leg over the sill, stopped and looked back over his shoulder and said, 'bless you preacher, sorry Von. I'll make it up to you."

He darted out the window, into the darkness of the meadow and disappeared.

Reverend Tallman hurried to the front of the church and placed his weapons by the door. Running to the wide path, leading to the road, he turned and ran away from the church and toward the forest and in the opposite direction Theo had gone. He dragged the shirt on the ground until he came to the bend in the creek and flung the shirt into the water. He turned and ran back to the steps of the church.

Von was nervously pacing in front of the church. He watched as Reverend Tallman ran back.

"What do you want me to do, preacher?" he said, when the minister returned.

The dogs were 150 yards from the church and coming fast. The men on horses, unable to come up the creek due to the treacherous terrain, had been forced to stay on the narrow road. The lights from their torches danced through the dark around the creek and up the road leading to the church.

Reverend Tallman stuck a revolver in his trousers and covered it with his shirt. He bent over and put the coal oil lamp he was carrying, on the ground. "All right boy, you listen close," he said, "you stand beside that door inside and be ready. If I yell, you throw this scattergun to me, than you get down on your belly and get behind a bench, you understand me?

"Yes, sir, I understand," Von said. "What about you, preacher, you're not staying out there, are you? You know preachers bleed like any other man."

The preacher waved him off, lit another coal oil lamp and placed it on a stump further away from the church. The sweat of the two men glistened in the light.

Von turned, went into the church and stood by the door. He kept it opened slightly, to see outside.

Reverend Josiah Tallman, late of the Confederate army, Minister of the Gospel. who only wanted to live his life for the Lord and to do God's work, repositioned the revolver in his waistband and turned toward the path. He faced the noisy bedlam of the pack of dogs that had quickly appeared out of the dark woods. The bouncing lights of torches, held by the men on horseback, turned the bend of the creek and moved toward the road that went by the church.

Von stood behind the church door and gripped the 10 gauge, double barrel, shotgun tightly. Although it was hard to breathe, he forced a big gulp of air into his lungs and slowly released it.

The howling, snarling, barking pack of large hounds, raised their noses from the ground when they saw the large man standing still in front of the lights shining in the darkness, surrounding the church. They ran toward the man and surrounded him on the flat ground.

Von Lucas rubbed his eyes to make sure he was not dreaming the scene in the lights of the lamps.

It was as if Reverend Tallman was totally unaware of the pack of dogs. His only movement was when he slowly raised one finger over the milling pack of animals, and held it high over their heads. Suddenly as if one body and one mind, the dozen or so dogs, immediately stopped barking, and sat on their haunches.

Panting. Tongues hanging out of their mouths. Not moving.

Even when Albert Jessel and a group of heavily armed riders, carrying torches, galloped into the clearing in front of the church, even then…the dogs stayed still … and quiet.

Von shuddered and fought hard not to pee on himself.

## Chapter Three-
## ...He that hath no gun...buy one.


Von Lucas knew, when he recognized most of the men, who rode into the clearing, this was no ordinary, riding in the dark, chasing petty chicken thieves, maybe whip, beat up or scare... kind of gang of men. The men, who rode into that church clearing, had reputations for doing more than patrolling the roads and enforcing Colonel Winston's law. These men were notorious in their cruelty and crimes against people of color. Drunk and out for fun, they had one united mission, to raise hell and... and to hurt people. Von knew them to be bad men. Very bad men.

He wondered why he didn't leave with Theo Cook, when Reverend Tallman told him to go. He didn't know that compelled him to stay. It wasn't courage. Von wasn't necessarily a brave man. He was like any other man, who just wanted to live and let live. Why? Why, he thought. WHY did he encounter Theo? WHY did he have to take that trail to the church? WHY didn't he keep runing, when he had the chance. Stupid. Stupid. Stupid... he thought.

His heart ached at the thought of Mary and the life they had planned together...

He tried to crouch lower behind the church door.

In the annuals of history, there are stories of battles between good and evil men. Through the centuries, one faction has never been able to eradicate the other. As a child, Von Lucas had learn early to recognize the difference between the cruelty of evil men, and the goodness of decent men... like his father and like Reverend Tallman.

When the light of the torches, they were carrying, revealed the faces of the men, riding into the church clearing, Von knew without a doubt, he was going to diethat night. He wondered if it was God's preplanned destiny, for him to die in a church. He felt anger, at the thought of God, leading him to this place, and causing him to be placed under the protection of Reverend Tallman. What was going to happen to Mary? Why? Why, God… on this night? Why?

When the riders stopped short, where the dogs lay in the dirt, the thought came to Von's mind. Evil has found me.

Evil on horseback.

The desperation and fear, rising in his chest, made it difficult for him to breathe… and to pray.

---

Albert Jessel was livid. He had not spent countless hours training his dogs, to suddenly have them lay down when the chase was almost over. Their job was to track and attack, causing their prey to climb a tree. His dogs were the best trained trackers in Georgia. Once they were on your trail, it was over. Just give up and hope for the best.

But now… his highly, prized dogs, were on their bellies, like house pets, waiting to be fed. Instead of attacking and treeing, they were panting and whining.

A tall black man, standing by several coal lamps, on the ground, had his head down, one hand in the air, as if praying. The dogs lay in front of him.

The riders thundered into the clearing on their tired

mounts, and came to a stop, reining in behind the dogs. Two riders stayed behind, at the edge of the path, to watch the main road.

Reverend Tallman raised his head, and lowered his arm. Like a trick in a traveling magic show, Von saw one time in Johnsonville, the dogs, immediately got up, and moved as one group, to the brush at the edge of the forest. Tame. Docile. The dogs, all sat and watched the large man of God, who suddenly had become the leader of the pack.

Albert Jessel did not want to call too much attention, to the other riders, at how his dogs were failing in their training, so he only swore at them under his breath. The big black man, standing in the light of the coal lamps, would pay for whatever he did to Albert's dogs. He would see to that.

Two of the riders broke ranks, and disappeared behind the church building.

With the addition of the torches, held by the riders, Von Lucas could see every feature of every man on horseback. He recognized two of the men immediately. One of them was Ollie Johnson, from east of Houston's Hollow. He was a small man, with narrow cheekbones, and slits for eyes. Everyone in the county knew Ollie. He was cruel and vicious and didn't particularly care how he made… or stoled money. His father had banned him from the family, and his General Store, for stealing.

The other man Von recognized, was Colonel Farrell Winston.

Colonel Winston was obviously the leader of the group, and out looking for a little fun and sport. Colonel Winston was bitter about the loss of the war and his generational and influential hold, on certain parts of, what he considered, proper, Southern society. He resented the necessity of former slaves, to work in his fields and the audacity of them to ask for wages to do the work. He made up for that resentment by having a few drinks and taking midnight rides for entertainment.

Von noticed how quiet it had become, other than the blowing of the lathered horses as they came to a stop.

It had been a long chase. He recognized other men in the group. Nod Washington, who ran the local cock fights, and was a cousin to Ollie Johnson, sat on a big roan gelding. He was like Ollie, and didn't care who he hurt, or what he had to do for some extra dollars in his pocket. Another, of the riders, was J.J. Smith, the son-in-law of Colonel Winston. He rode a black filly and had a shotgun strapped to his back.

Though the crack, Von counted five men in the clearing in front of the church, two men had stayed back at the edge of the path, leading to the road, and two that had disappeared behind the church. That made nine. Nine men. Not very good odds he thought. Please God, help us. He hoped the men outside couldn't hear his heart pounding in his chest.

Colonel Winston prompted his horse to stop in front of Reverend Tallman. He took a deep breath, looked around the church clearing, then turned his eyes back toward the preacher. This was sport to him. He enjoyed the chase, the barking hounds, and the torches. But, more than anything else, he enjoyed seeing the fear in the eyes of his quarry. Chicken and pig thieves were almost a necessary to the Colonel's lifestyle, to add some excitement to an otherwise boring life. There was nothing more enjoyable to the Colonel, and his men, then turning up a couple of bottles of whiskey, and chase somebody down… and hurt them. They always found somebody, for the dogs to pursue. But this chase had been longer and more tedious than Colonel Winston had anticipated. He was hot. He was tired

Colonel Winston chose each word carefully, when he finally spoke. Von could see the Colonel was doing his best to scare and intimidate the Reverend Tallman. Put him in his place, first. That was what was important to Colonel Farrell Winston.

He spoke down to Reverend Tallman.

"Mister,' he said, 'I assume you are responsible for Mr. Jessel's critters acting like a bunch of lap puppies, and I assume by the way they are acting, you are not the person we seek. We are looking for the son-of-a-bitches who's been helping themselves to my property. Namely my pigs and my chickens. They're in the church, right? You might as well tell them to come on out. Who are you, anyway?"

Ollie Johnson, looking for favor, kneed his horse forward and stopped beside the Colonel.

"That's the new preacher, Colonel,' he said,' He hadn't been here but a couple months. Tallman? That's your name, ain't it preacher, Tallman? You fought at Manassas, didn't you? Some folks say you wore grey, but fought for the blue. Maybe a spy or something like that." He turned and faced the Colonel. "Anyway, that's what some folks say," he said.

Winston acknowledged Ollie, with a slight nod of his head. He said, " Thank you, Mister Johnson, for that information." He turned and waited for Reverend Tallman to respond.

Inside the darkness of the church, Von marveled at the preacher's courage, standing in front of the of the five night riders. He felt his knees start to knock together. He could feel the heat from the torches, the riders carried outside the church. Sweat poured off his brow, into his eyes. He thought of Mary, and again for the hundredth time, he felt regret, he didn't run with Theo. He probably would have been home by now. He prayed for God's protection, under his breath.

The preacher stood erect and was smiling, when he finally broke his silence. Reverend Tallman's calming, bass, voice, had a welcoming tone. Each word, raised and lowered in pitch, each sentence an instrument, almost like a song… as if he was standing behind the pulpit on Sunday morning. As he spoke, he turned his head both ways and looked directly in the eye of each of the men, surrounding him. He was unafraid.

"Welcome. I am Reverend Josiah Tallman. I am pastor and protector of this church and of my flock. … and to answer my brother, (he motioned at Ollie Johnson), as a lowly sinner, I fell at Manassas," he said," but, Jesus gave me a new life… Hallelujah, as a servant of the holy word. And in the spirit of my faith, as a sign of friendship and hospitality, and as Jesus commanded … I ask, how may I help you, brethren? Can I offer you food or drink?

He picked up the coal oil lamps, and motioned the men closer, a welcoming smile on his face.

Von's heart sank. He thought, it sounded almost like the preacher was inviting the wolves into the sheep's pen. Please God. Please God…save us sweet Jesus, he suddenly had another terrifying thought, the preacher was acting like he WANTED the men there. Why? No, it couldn't be. But, what if…? Panic. He felt betrayed. Don't panic. Breathe. Just Breathe. What was Reverend Tallman thinking? Was he surrendering? Was it a trap? Was this planned somehow?

The two riders, who had disappeared behind the church building, rode out of the darkness and rejoined the other men.

One of the riders with a large brim hat, rode up to Colonel Winston. "No sign in back I can see, Colonel, there's a false trail headed to the creek " he said," He's in the church, I'm sure."

Von's felt sick when he suddenly recognized the man speaking.

Jackson George. The overseer and personal bulldog of Colonel Farrell Winston, was well known throughout the valleys and ridges of North Georgia. The meanest and most violent man in the county. He had beaten, shot or hung people of color under the pretense of the law, and orders from Colonel Winston. The local sheriff overlooked George's actions, due to Winston's influence. Most people, in Stuart County, used the Devil's and Jackson George's name, to scare their children into behaving.

Colonel Winston, arrogantly and impatiently, slapped his hand on his side.

"Blue-belly spy, huh?" he said, nodding affirmably to the other men, and turning his head to spit on the ground, "Well, imagine that. We can talk about that later, What I do know is, I know, we didn't come here for no damn sermon… right now, anybody in that church building better get themselves out here…NOW!" he yelled at the church building, his voice cracking in anger, at being denied his sport. He put his free hand on the flap, covering the pistol in the belt on his side.

Von crouched down by the door. He could see Reverend Tallman, standing with the coal lanterns, outstretched from his body, raise his head upward. His lips were moving. Praying.

Von could not hear him plainly, but it sounded like he was saying the word… Azrael? It was something like that, Von couldn't tell. The preacher's voice was low. Pleading.

"While he's talking to God, put some holes in that building, force that bastard out," Colonel Winston said, pulling the pistol from his flapped, holster on his side.

Von Lucas saw the men move away from Reverend Tallman, and spread out in the church clearing. He quickly pulled a church bench over and fell down behind it, just as the men began firing rifles and pistols, at the church. Glass from other windows fell under the barrage of bullets.

After the men emptied their guns, they reloaded and fired again, until empty once more.

J.J. Smith, son-in-law of Colonel Winston and largest moonshine provider, to those in the county, who liked a taste, enjoyed these midnight rides immensely. He considered cruelty, as gauge in winning favor in his father's-in-law eyes. He took a swig, moved his horse to the side of the church and threw his torch onto the roof. "I'll help them to see their way out," he laughed, to the Colonel," Come on boys, lets light this old building up!" He motioned to Jackson George and to the men beside him. The other two riders who had been watching the road, turned and galloped their horses to the church, to join the fun.

There had been rain the day before, and Von had a hopeful thought that the roof shingles, of the church, would be slow to start burning.

The thought didn't last long.

"Let me show you how to build a fire," said Nod Washington, riding past J.J., and throwing his torch through a plane glass window of the church. The fire started to spread quickly, above the window frame, and to the inside rafters.

It quickly became a whirlwind of dust outside, as horses spun around to clear space for other riders to toss torches at the building. The church clearing was lit by coal oil lamps, torches, and the church fire, and above the treetops an encircling ring of smoke, from gunpowder and wet wood, begin to form.

These men did not want to talk anymore.

Von felt panic at the spreading fire above him. He was going to have to run for it. He marveled at Reverend Tallman. The tall man stood, holding the lanterns out from his side, and watching the riders and horses, moving around in the church clearing. He did not seem concerned about any danger he was in. He did not move.

"If that thief is not out in one minute, shoot this man." said Colonel Winston, motioning to Reverend Tallman and reloading his revolver, "let's be done with it." It angered him that the preacher did not back away or show any fear. The black man calmly stood there, holding the lanterns up .

Von Lucas watched through the cracked church door, and he felt his muscles tightening and starting to cramp. Whatever was going to happen is getting ready to start. He knew he was going to burn alive in the church or be shot if he stepped outside, he was a dead man either way. He thought about Mary and his love for her… oh, God, oh God, he whispered, give me strength and power. Save us, oh sweet Lord.

It was the prayer of desperation. A prayer for a miracle.

Von Lucas knew he, and the preacher, were going to die.

Too many men. No escape. He gripped the shotgun tightly …ready to throw it if the preacher yelled. He covered his mouth with the front of his shirt, trying to breathe through the smoke, from the wet wood Oh, God, he thought, what to do…yell. Don't yell. wait…Yell. No. Run. Don't run.

Reverend Tallman started to pray in his deep powerful voice, and despite the rampage of the fire above him, Von Lucas started to relax and feel his cramped muscles ease a little. The sound of the preacher had a plea and rhythm that reverberated throughout the clearing, and seemed enhanced by the growing flames in the top of the church. Von started to feel a strange sensation on his skin, like he was actually being caught up in the pull from earth, to heaven, as Reverend Tallman talked to God. He pulled the shirt away from his face. He didn't need it to breathe anymore, even though the church was filling with smoke.

"My savior," said Reverend Tallman, prayed as he turned and faced the riders, who had gathered in front of him to see him shot . "Oh, my savior. The God of **Azrael**, once more… I ask …for help. Oh my God, show them the power of **Azrael,** thy chosen angel."

His prayer, mingled in with the echoes of his voice in the church clearing, and supported by the fire and smoke from the church building, became a choir of prayers, thrown to the sky… and it seemed to Von Lucas's frantic mind, with such intensity in nature, Reverend Tallman's prayer had to have landed at the feet of God Almighty, himself.

As the fervent prayer was lifted to the heavens, Von started to feel a transformation in his breathing. He started to feel calmer, although his senses seemed heightened. Whatever was going to happen, he knew he would be ready. It was as if his adrenaline had suddenly harnessed four more horses to his plow. He felt an odd sense of power in his legs, as he straightened from his crouch in the dark of the church. Something strange was happening to his body.

A crash of thunder exploded in the sky above the clearing. It started to rain. An intricate design of light appeared, as a bolt of lighting streaked across the night sky. A slow drizzle, then harder. A full fledge downpour of large raindrops, in seconds, causing the fire on the roof to smolder, with thick smoke billowing into the air.

The large man of God, stood there with the coal lamps held out to his sides and rain pouring off his face. He looked at Colonel Winston with defiance in his eyes, .

"Judgement day," said Reverend Tallman, "it's your judgement day."

"Shoot this man, shoot him now, and bury him where we stand," Colonel Winston, said angrily and abruptly,"Let's be done with it. I'm through wasting time." He turned the reins quickly and cut his horse out of the line of fire, and to the rear of the group.

Jackson George, grinned, and raised his rifle toward Reverend Tallman.

"Come oooonn, **Azrael**," Reverend Tallman yelled, and suddenly threw the coal lamps at the feet of the horses, causing them to rear and buck away in terror, making their riders forget their guns, and grab their saddle horns to keep from being thrown. The startled dogs jumped up from where they were laying, and disappeared into the thick bush, underneath the trees around the clearing.

Instintively, as soon as Von Lucas saw the coal lamps leave the preacher's hands, he swung the church door open, and pitched the shotgun toward the reverend. It flew through the air directly into the preacher's waiting hands.

This is it, Von thought.

It was strange he thought… he felt no fear. He reached down and unconsciously, picked up the lever action Winchester, leaning on the wall next to him.

He felt detached. He felt like he was in a dream, slow moving in a cloud, almost….graceful, out of his control, each movement planned in advance…He felt something moving him. Directing him. it wasn't his arms, his legs...his hands. It was something else. Something very powerful.

Jackson's George's horse had almost thrown him off initially, but the man held on and brought his rifle back up one handed, and fired at Reverend Tallman, hitting him in the knee and knocking him down.

Reverend Josiah Tallman, the man of peace...fell to the ground, wounded, then in one reflexive motion, Reverend Tallman, the former soldier, whirled on his good knee, and pulled both triggers of the 10 gauge shotgun, pointed at Jackson George.

Jackon George, fell backwards, and disappeared off his horse in a booming cloud of smoke and powder. His horse bolted from the clearing, and ran back to the path toward the road.

The other riders, managed to get control of their horses quickly after the shotgun blast, and each turned toward the down minister, bringing their revolvers or rifles to bear. Colonel Winston reined in his horse and headed back toward the fallen Reverend Tallman, who was lying in front of the church, his leg bleeding profusely. Ollie Johnson jerked his horse around violently, his face twisted in a vengeful anger. The other riders kept their fingers on the trigger of their guns, hate and murder mirrored in their eyes...and moved in toward the downed preacher.

Reverend Tallman was struggling to pull the revolver from the waistband of his pants.

Colonel Winston stopped his horse, and looked down at Reverend Tallman.

"You're a dead man," he said, pulling his revolver and pointing it at the fallen pastor.

Ollie Johnson saw Albert Jessel plummet backwards and disappear off from his horse, and was the first of the group, in the pouring down rain, to distinguish the difference between the bluish light coming from the church door, and the reddish light of the fire inside the church's rooftop, and the remaining torches held by the riders. He thought it odd, the approaching light was enhanced by smaller extensions of multiple red lights, and then he realized the explosions he was hearing, matched the flames from the end of the rifle barrel, being fired by Von Lucas.

Colonel Winston saw the movement of light next, and turned and pointed his pistol at Von. Ollie Johnson saw a blur as Von's hand, levered a shell into the chamber and shot Colonel Winston through the head. Ollie Johnson had never seen anything like it in his life, in or around Stuart County. He knew it was not humanly possible to shoot a gun like that... and he didn't know a black man in these parts, even knew HOW to hold a repeating rifle... much less, shoot it.

Von walked as if in a trance, his features and body emitting a strange blue light. He was holding the rifle by his side, levering the action quickly, shooting each man off his horse in rapid succession. Nod Washington went to meet his maker as he tried to cock his pistol. J.J. Smith went to hell, with his mouth twisted in surprise. The riders were frozen in motion, because of what they were witnessing. They were not aware, the vengeful figure, bathed in blue light, and shooting a Winchester rifle, would be the last thing they ever saw.

Ollie Johnson turned his horse and kicked him into a dead run toward the road. The terrified horse needed no further encouragement to escape the fire and explosions. Ollie gave the horse his head and galloped through the rain, back onto the road and the safety of darkness.

Reverend Tallman looked at Von, approaching him. A bluish halo of light surrounded the young man and glistened in the falling water of the rain, and the glow of the church fire. The wounded pastor lay back on the ground, holding his bleeding leg.

"**Azrael**," he said, to nobody particular… since everybody around him, was dead.

A powerful blast of wind and rain, blew through the clearing, forcing the rain water to stream through the windows and bullet holes, in the walls of the Ebenezer African Methodist Church, with such force, it extinguished the fire throughout the House of the Lord… another gust of wind blew, whatever remaining smoke from the blaze, out through the broken glass windows and cleared the sanctuary.

**Azrael**… the **Angel of God**…the **Angel of Death**, moved and stood protectively over the fallen Reverend Tallman. The Winchester rifle was still smoking.

## Chapter Four
## Conclusion
### 'Covered by the blood of Jesus'

Reverend Josiah Tallman jerked himself back to reality, and from the memory of that night long ago. He wiped the tears from his eyes and stood from the church bench where he had been praying. He watched through the window, and thought of Ollie Johnson.

Ollie had escaped that night and had died an old man in a state institution. He had needed constant care and had not been able to speak because of the horrific trauma, caused by Azrael. Any form of communication from Ollie, involved grunts and gibberish on his part, since he had never learned to write and his brain capacity seemed to have reverted to that of a small child. Reverend Tallman had prayed for him every day he had been alive.

Reverend Tallman spent most of his time in prayer and penance, after killing Jackson George that night. God allowed him to visit the old church every year, and pray for atonement for that sin. It was a time for rejoicing at God's power, but it was also a time of sadness because of the memory.

The old man, started to move toward the door. It was time to go. Through the window, he saw a cute little girl, standing in front of the table where the biscuits and gravy had been placed. She was smiling and waving at him. He waved back, touched with the innocence and beauty of the child.

Outside under the oak tree, Von Lucas had gingerly put Mary, his great-granddaughter, down, when she started showing impatience at being held so long. She was wanting a biscuit, out of a basket on a nearby table, and was determined to get it no matter how hard she had to struggle or loud she had to yell. After he put her down, a few seconds passed before she realized she had her freedom and she suddenly got quiet. Distracted by something out of Von's vision, she seemed to forget about the biscuit, and started looking intently past the tables and tree. Von glanced where she was looking, toward the front of the old church at the edge of the property and the large flower garden.

It had been a rush burial, but Theo Cooker and several of the menfolk, had come to help that night, and dug the necessary graves so deep, no one would want to put in the amount of work, needed to find them. They never spoke about that night the rest of their lives.

No-one ever knew or even suspected, Colonel Winston, and the other missing men, of Stuart County, had ended up underneath the church yard of Ebenezer African Methodist Church. Countless search parties, from the Army and local law, had ridden horses and wagons over the burial site so much, they had erased any detectable sign of the graves. Wicked men had been dealt with by God in Stuart County, Johnsonville, Georgia that night, and they were buried where they stood.

Only Von, and Reverend Tallman, knew that Azrael the Angel of Death, had been sent by God to protect them that night. They both felt the assurance of God, they were doing his will, and that their sins were covered by the blood of Jesus, and heaven would be their reward. People, of the community, had heard rumors of Von's prowess with a rifle, but no one could ever recollect of ever seeing him shoot a gun anyplace, or anytime, for that matter. Everyone knew Von and his wife, Mary, and their family, as stalwart pillars of the community, who always helped others, and were friends and supporters of the church and it's missions.

Von's thoughts, of Reverend Tallman, always left a warm glow in his chest, when he thought about his mentor and pastor. He enjoyed these 'Tallman Day' Celebration's every year and was often asked to tell of the history of the old church to the younger members. Reverend Tallman had always been a beacon of love, and an example of service to others, and how a man should walk and live in his faith to God Almighty. It was rightfully so, Von thought, the old preacher should be honored this way.

Reverend Tallman, standing in the window, made a funny face at the little girl, then smiled, and waved at her with two large hands.

Mary, no longer cranky and impatient, was laughing at the man in the window. She pointed at him, and waved back.

She was happy and content. "Look Papa Von," she said, pointing at the old church window, "big man, big man,"

Looking up at the empty window, and seeing nothing, Von Lucas, took his great-granddaughter's hand, and headed her toward the biscuit table.

"Come on, child," he said, "let's say the blessing and eat."

**the end**

# The Healing Stream

## Chapter One - Falling Off A Mountain

The flashing engine light took my attention from the mountains and the three hundred foot drop on the other side of the guardrail. I gripped the steering wheel a little tighter with my good hand and looked ahead to pull over.

My new Rover was overheating.

I said a word my Mother wouldn't like. It was under my breath for sure, but she still wouldn't have like it.

I had just taken the vehicle in for the six month service check last week and the flashing light was totally unexpected. I shrugged my shoulders in acceptance of the moment. If I couldn't fix it, it wouldn't be the first time I had to walk or march somewhere.

In my youth and naiveté, I once ignored bright, red lights flashing on the dash and ended up with a blown engine, much to the chagrin of my Mother and Uncle Paul. Considering, I had learned my lesson many years ago and the Rover was fairly new and expensive, as soon as I came to a small parking area beside the road, I pulled that baby over.

I put the shift in Park, rolled the window down and turned the engine off.

Taking in a deep breath of fresh, crisp mountain air, I held it in my lungs like I had just hit the bong my cousin use to keep out in the old outhouse where we use to play. The mountain air…ahhhh, I loved it. I savored the aroma and taste of the air and held on to it until it was time to take another breath. Air, in higher altitudes, seems to have a special fragrance of its own. At least I think that's the case in the mountains of my ancestors located in East Tennessee. It's a mixture of plant and animal life mingled with woodsmoke and corn mash. A bouquet of mystery permeated with thousands of years of being formed into being part of nature's skyline.

I stepped out of the Rover and took a quick look at the surrounding terrain. It was just a cleared spot on the highway through the mountains. I've passed it countless times in my travels to Jarman Hollow, although I couldn't remember ever stopping here before. On the North side of the road was a steep incline toward North Carolina. On the South side of the road, was a wider area with guardrails made of old railroad ties. They were lined beside the road and separated the asphalt from a gradual cliff one or two hundred feet below. There were rows of trees and brush, behind the guardrail, which multiplied quickly until merging into an indistinguishable curtain of foliage.

The Great Smokey Mountains or Shaconage 'place of the blue smoke' as called by the Cherokee Indians, native tribe to the region, has been home for families of Scottish decent since the late 1790s. Heritage runs deep in the DNA of my people and the land where my ancestors settled.

The roots of the stories passed through the families, have a rich and diverse history. Some are based on Indian folklore, with tales of Indian spirits that once walked the Earth, other stories are regaled as family history and are mixed with mountain lore and ancient tales. Different versions of the same story are told depending on their Scottish lineage. Stories have been used not only to inform and educate, but to also entertain and scare children sitting around fireplaces through the generations. Unbelievable tales about fire breathing panthers, ghostly warriors appearing on full moon nights or unexplained happenings involving owls and crows, were the types of anecdotes handed down. Every ridge and hollow of any name it seemed, had a witch or 'special' lady, capable of bad or good luck omens with incantations and potions to affect enemies for a price. They were real and not to be ignored, according to the older mountain people.

To anyone who might doubt a tale's authenticity, blood relatives would swear its validity with hands on family bibles. I could listen to my Uncle Paul talk for hours about stories his grandfather had told him... there was no doubt in my mind everything was true.

Thinking of Uncle Paul, reminded me I better get on the move and see what the problem is with my Rover.

The shadows of late afternoon, underneath the Tennessee canopy of trees, were something to consider and I really didn't want to be on the narrow road any longer than necessary. The area was isolated and desolate in some parts and phone service was always sketchy. Traveling through the valleys and ridges of the Great Smokey Mountains was always risky if you needed to communicate with the outside world.

I walked to the front of the Rover and struggled to open the hood. The cast on my left hand and the arm sling around my neck made it difficult to grasp the hood firmly enough to pull it up. Grunting from the pain at the stress on the broken bones, I took my arm out of the sling and managed to hoist the hood up and over my head using both hands.

Knowing what was coming, I stood there for a minute with both arms up in the air, holding onto the hood. The blood flowing back into my left arm brought waves of pain, from the injured nerves. I tried to control my breathing to lessen the agony. I noticed blood had leaked through the cast. That wasn't a good sign.

It had been four weeks since my hand and arm had been crushed, pushing a school bus stuck out of the mud on the side of the road. The driver had gone in reverse when I yelled 'Give it all you got'. Unfortunately, I meant go forward and I was caught between the bus's bumper and a steel guardrail. After countless apologies, a Good Samaritan write-up in the school and local newspaper, two surgeries and a tub full of pain pills, I had finally felt like getting back to work.

Work meant driving through the mountains.

So, here I am.

Looking under the Rover's hood at the water reservoir leading to the radiator, I saw it was bone dry. The radiator was steaming.

I shook my head and took another look around the road and the area where I was parked.

Nothing.

The last Ma and Pa grocery store/gas station was back down the mountain at least 14 miles. I was just two miles from my destination and getting water seemed to be the only problem.

The sound of a bird, cawing deep in the forest, filtered through the tall trees surrounding the road. The bird's cackles faded to silence and everything else grew still. There was no sign of any traffic on the curvy, mountain road. The faint rumble of a waterfall, came from somewhere past the railroad ties down toward the ravine. My labored breathing, as I tried to mentally control the shooting pains in my hand, was the only other sound.

Looking back at the radiator, I saw the steam blowing into the air was slowing to a low hiss. The cap looked lopsided and maybe was not on properly. Or so it seemed, I was not about to take it off and have it explode in my face.

This was not the first time I had driven this road. I knew it well. I pretty much had grown up in this area.

Every month I come back to the birthplace of my

Mother's people to replenish my supply of Paul's 'special' nectar of the mountains. I guess people would call me a wholesaler, if you had to put a label on my job description.

'Paul's Tennessee Finest,' is a mountain made moonshine whiskey, and although it is produced in some of the worst terrain on Earth, the golden liquid was once described by one of European nobility, that 'if taste buds could recognize holy comparisons, this is how one would imagine heaven might taste'.

This 'not so' secret drink of the upper echelons of wealth, around the world, is produced and sold by my Uncle Paul Stonewall.

Over the years and through the genius of his marketing, Uncle Paul's moonshine had become a much sought after commodity throughout the inner circles of some of the wealthiest names and families in Russia, Europe, South America and the United State. Paul's Tennessee Finest (PTF) whiskey was established as a benchmark of wealth and status. Clients pay a high price to exclusively serve genuine PTF ... each relishing in the notoriety of being able to offer it straight from their own personal liquor cabinet, and being able to retell stories about Paul Stonewall and his legendary drink. The taste is said to be so memorable because of the mountain spring water used in distillation and is so distinct, it's never been duplicated. Each person who has ever participated in a Paul's Tennessee Finest tasting, appreciates the rarity and the difficulty in obtaining this memorable drink... and pays a high price to do so and tell about it.

I turned and tried to focus in on the sound of the waterfall I heard in the distance. That was the only choice I had, to get water from whatever resources were close by.

The faint roar of water seemed to be coming from literally just past the first line of trees toward the ravine. I walked past the ties and the edge of the road. Something under a near bush caught my eye. A narrow animal trail, with natural steps from erosion and exposed tree roots, started and curved downward into the thick mountain brush. Standing on the first step, I clearly heard the intermittent sounds of water flowing below.

Excited at an easy solution to my problem, I hurriedly walked back to the Rover. I opened the hatch and retrieved an empty 5 Gallon plastic container from the twenty containers strapped and banded together in the back of the vehicle.

I was sure I could carry the five gallon load with my good hand and it should be all the water I needed to fill the radiator and reservoir.

I had another two miles before I got off the main road. My destination was an old logging road that's just two runs in the dirt through the woods. Only country folk would call it a road. City folk would call it a suicide circus ride. Generations of Stonewalls had liked the difficulty and seclusion of the terrain and called it home. The natural positioning of the mountains creates shadows along the ridges of Jarman Hollow that makes any type of modern satellite imaging virtually impossible. Neighbors in these mountains are ten miles apart as a crow flies, and fifteen miles if you can get around with a horse, mule or some type of ATV. The older folks only see each other at revivals, funerals and pig killings.

My Mother, Ruth Margaret Stonewall and Paul Stonewall were brother and sister and had grown up together in Jarman Hollow. My Dad met my Mom, stole her heart and they moved to Knoxville to live. After I was born my Dad left for Viet Nam and didn't come back. My

Mother decided to stay in Knoxville and Uncle Paul started taking me every summer back to the mountains and taught me to do all kinds of things, like how to track, hunt and fish, and how to make moonshine whiskey... (although my Mother never approved of the last part).

After a four year stint with the Army's 101st Airborne and unsure about college or a career when I got out, Uncle Paul offered me a job working for him. At first, selling and marketing Uncle Paul's moonshine, was only going to be a stepping stone until I decided on a more 'Mom Approved,' acceptable career path, I thought so anyway... the money and lifestyle that followed my decision to work for Uncle Paul was unimaginable. Mom ultimately benefited from my decision and after a while you would have thought it was her idea to take the job. I just closed on a vacation house in Florida for her and my sister last month. After the rough time Mom has been having with the cancer and surgery the past year, I felt good about being able to do that for her. I knew they were having a good time, soaking up the sun and being as carefree as possible.

Right now though, money was not going to help me get any water... I had one good hand and I needed to hurry up as signs of evening could come quickly over the tree tops. Bears live in these mountains and could be bothersome if you didn't keep your guard up. I reached in the glove compartment and retrieved the holster holding my .45 Ruger. With one hand in a cast, I clumsily pulled and checked the clip of hollow points, slipped the clip back, put a round in the chamber and made sure the safety was on. Clipping the holster to my belt, I latched the gun in place, close to my good hand.

I had an empty, leather-wrapped whiskey flask in the console I was going to give to Uncle Paul as a present. On a whim, I picked it up and jammed it in my rear pocket. If I got thirsty, it would be nice to have a smaller container to drink from. Cold, clear water running straight out of the mountain, is the cleanest and best drinking water on the planet.

The stream sounded close so I was sure I wasn't going to be gone that long.

The sound of the bird started back, his cawing from the trees was closer as I stepped off the road and down the short embankment into the tree line. The bird's calls echoed off rock walls and huge trees. It was an eerie sound that dissipated into the forest. Then once again, silence.

The trail was fairly easy walking, with little dense undergrowth or thickets to smack you in the face. The incline toward the bottom was not as steep as it seemed looking from the top of the road.

Each step downhill reminded me of my broken and scarred hand. It's hard to bend your knees when you walk downhill. Being able to bend my knees would have cushioned the natural impact of walking, which would have been easier on my hand. Each step was stiff-legged and jarring. The doctors had said it would probably be two more operations and five to ten more metal screws, before I regained any mobility in my fingers. The nerves, tendons and bones had been smashed flat as an Aunt Jemima pancake.

I stopped for a moment to catch my breath and leaned on a huge Oak tree beside the trail. I released the arm sling and held my injured hand above my shoulder to relieve the pressure of the cast. The blood stain was getting larger.

Walking on down the trail, I zig zagged back and forth into the forest. The possibility of being lost never really crossed my mind. I knew I was heading south and in the general direction of Jarman Hollow. The water I was trying to find was probably a tributary of the main source for Paul Stonewall's moonshine still operation.

The trail became wider abruptly and stopped at a large open point overlooking a huge ravine. A large stream of whitewater, flowed from the top of the surrounding mountain above me, and formed a pond about fifty feet below me. The pool of water had a golden hue highlighted by the sunlight, slipping through the trees on the horizon. There were strange shadows with a bluish tint, formed by the ripples caused by the waterfall's force as it crashed on the surface. The water in the pool overflowed the shoreline on the farthest edge and continued until disappearing into the valley farther below the plateau of the pool. Leaning over the edge of the embankment I was standing on, I was able to see where the trail continued and meandered to the pool. It wasn't that far. I could be back up in a minute.

Turning to continue down the trail, I froze.

A bear had come in behind me and was standing thirty feet from me.

Just standing.

Staring at me intently.

He wrinkled his nose like he picking up a scent. I noticed the blood on my cast where my hand had started bleeding. That was how the bear hooked onto me. The blood. Anything is possible with a big black bear.

I hesitated to reached for my gun, but pulled it from my holster just in case. I wasn't crazy. I really didn't want to shoot a bear. That might raise all kinds of questions if discovered.

In the Army, I had been in combat situations and

had been scared out of my mind most of those times. I don't mind admitting it. Training becomes instinct though, so I took a deep breath and tried to stay calm.

I wasn't scared out of my mind yet, but I was definitely concerned.

I gripped the gun a little tighter.

I took a quick glance over my shoulder at the waterfall and the pool behind me. Wow, that's a long way to go. I mentally gauged the distance and angle the bear had on me to the trail leading down to the pool. Twenty feet and he would be on me. Couldn't go that way.

The bear snarled and took a step toward me.

I have encountered black bears before. I know what the books say to do. Don't run. Don't show fear. Make noise. Appear as large as possible. Don't Play dead. Fight like hell. All kinds of things one can do when confronting a bear. Oh, and be sure to PRAY was something I heard Uncle Paul say one time. Don't forget to pray.

I also knew each situation is always different and you have to go on what your gut tells you.

The bear lowered his head and took a step in my direction. My gut told me this bear was thinking about eating me so I went ahead and said the prayer Uncle Paul had recommended.

I put the plastic container under my injured arm and pounded on it with the gun, yelling at the top of my voice.

Stepping to the side to get a better foothold, I tripped on an exposed root and fell backwards. Landing hard, the cast on my arm struck a rock and broke away from my hand, ripping bone fragments from metal screws sutures in my hand. The plastic container popped out from under my arm and bounced off the ridge and disappeared from view. I heard it hitting therocks along side the cliff, surrounding the pool of water below.

The bear jumped a step toward me and stopped. He was zoned in on me. Predator and prey. His brown eyes were intense and deadly. I could see the muscles in his haunches tighten. I knew what was coming. I slid the safety off the gun with my thumb.

I scooted my feet, backpedalling quickly and pointing the gun into the bear's face.

The bear charged, snarling and growling toward me. He stood on his back legs, reaching out with dagger like claws. His lips were pulled back, showing large canine teeth.

His charge pushed me backwards and I tripped on another branch. A rush of panic gripped my chest. I was running out of real estate.

The momentum of his charge pushed both of us over the edge of the cliff. As I fell backwards, I tried keeping him away from me with my feet and pulled the trigger as fast as I could, firing the gun into the bear's opened mouth, spewing blood and brain matter into the air as we both hurled toward the water.

Luckily, I cleared the rocks jutting under and away from the front of the cliff. The bear's body ricocheted heavily off a huge bolder and flew off to the side.

I marveled at the golden glitter of the water as it danced in the falling sunlight and rose to meet me.

Through gritted teeth, I braced for impact.

# Chapter Two
# 'Dead Bear Walking'

As I fell, I could see the large bear falling to the side of me, silhouetted against the sky. I knew the bear was dead. His body had gone limp immediately.

I hit the water hard.

The force of the landing knocked the breath out of me. My head spun from the impact and I felt I was on the edge of blacking out. Drifting underwater for a second, I groggily evaluated my physical condition. Other than my left hand and arm, nothing else seemed to be messed up. Everything else seemed to be working.

Thankfully, the depth of the water was deep enough not to hit bottom. I was ten feet under when I started clawing my way back to the surface. The pool was not that big in diameter though, maybe sixty foot. I floated and dog paddled with my good hand toward the low lying bank. Within a few feet I touched bottom and was able to walk toward the shore. The Northern bank opened up to a bank, covered with the greenest and softest moss I had ever seen.

Everything had happened so fast, I was just starting to feel the adrenaline kick in. I reached the shoreline but kept my body submerged. The cool temperature of the water was numbing the pain in my arm.

The water felt different for some reason.

Heavier...

The image of bathing in pure, clear honey, dripping from a shower, popped into my head.

Wow, too many pain pills, I thought.

The cold water trickled down from my hair into my eyes. Soothing to the touch, the texture was hard to describe, somehow it felt different, but it was still water.

Above, the waterfall's flow from the side of the mountain, was also very different then hundreds of other waterfalls, as it was intermittent and would go from a heavy stream to small flowing trickles into the pool below. It was like somebody was turning a faucet on and off and controlling the flow.

The water around me was turning red with the blood coming from my hand. On the other side of the pool where the bear's body floated, the water was crimson and spreading rapidly. The back of the bear's head had been blown away. Hollow points will do that. The bear's limp body bobbed up and down, where it was wedged under a downed tree sticking halfway out of the water.

The waterfall trickled to a drip… and then nothing.

A large crow landed in a clump of Maple trees at the edge of the golden pool of water. It flew from branch to branch in a flurry of feathers and wings. Evidently the gunshots and all the commotion had upset him. The excited bird started a consistent caw that was almost like the beating of a drum. The sound filled the area around the pool and expanded upwards in volume and frequency. It was getting on my nerves.

The transparent 5 gallon container was floating stationary, bumping into plant roots along the embankment next to the moss covered shoreline. I made my way over beside it and stopped to catch my breath.

Starting to pull myself upright, I suddenly felt faint and weak from shock.

My body was still immersed in the cool mountain water when I felt a boiling sensation shoot through my veins.

A burning pain coursed a path through the nerve center of my elbow and into the center of my core. It was like a hot ember from an open campfire. The sensation was unbearable and indescribable as I arched my back, feeling and seeing the bones moving around in my hand. My head spun in circles and it was hard to focus my eyes. I felt ligaments and tendons melding together, changing in shape and form. The skin on my hand moved with fluidity as it rippled and stretched into grotesque shapes.

I bent over, holding my hand between my knees. Over and over the bolt of excruciating pain came in agonizing waves, shooting through my hand and arm.

> Over and Over.
> Harder. More intense… and then.

> Gone.

> Just like that.
> The pain was gone.
> Gone. Nada.
> Total instant relief. It was crazy.

What was going on?
Breathing hard, I looked at my hand. It took a second to focus my eyes and comprehend at what I was seeing. A long, slow gasp of amazement escaped my clenched jaws.

> My hand was perfect.
> No blood.
> No stitches. No sutures.

The protruding bones in my palm had disappeared and back into my hand. No evident scars were visible from the traumatic injury.

It was perfect.

I cocked my head like a Cocker Spaniel and turned my miraculous hand over, front to back, front to back, front to back, trying to see it better. I shook my arm and wagged my hand hard in the air, trying to make the pain come back. That would let me know I wasn't dreaming. I let out another breath of bewilderment.

A loud snarl came from under the tree on the other side of the pool.

To my horror, there was movement in the water where the dead bear had been floating just moments ago.

The bear was on all fours in shallow water.

Very much alive.

He pitched and jerked his front claws and splashed the water violently, shaking his head side to side. Exposing his large teeth with each deep growl, he raked his long claws into the downed tree, taking out deep chunks of bark and turning it into kindling.

I frantically looked for my gun.

It was nowhere to be seen.

The angry bear stood upright on his back legs in the shallows of the water and howled a challenge into the air. He was in immense pain. I had just put a .45 hollow point through his brain, but now, there was no blood. No damage. Nothing but huge teeth, sharp claws and a pissed off attitude.

Again, I frantically looked around for my gun. It must have been knocked loose in the fall. I didn't see it anywhere. It was hard to look for it and watch the bear at the same time.

The bear was bellowing his growls and bashing his head back side to side. Pushing the tree away, he moved through the water with powerful front paws, got to the shore and lumbered toward me.

He had me.
There was no where to go.
The crow, whose consistent crowing had been a soundtrack to this whole dream-like scenario playing out, suddenly swooped down, frantically flapping both wings into the bears face and viciously nipping at his nose and eyes with a sharp beak.

The bear stopped and took a step backward. The bizarre attack clearly surprised him...as well as me.

The crow flew over his head, stopped in midair and swooped down like a kamikaze, repeatedly, hitting the bear in the face and diverting his attention.

I turned my head quickly, looking for the fastest way to escape this angry bear. A bright metallic reflection on the shoreline rocks near me, caught my eye.

It was my gun, caught in a nearby rock. If I moved a couple of feet I thought I might be able to stretch close enough to pick it up.

I took another quick look at the bear before I turned to get the gun.

I stopped at the sight of the bear and the diving crow.

The bear had backed up to the path and away from the attacking bird.

He shook his massive head, turned away from the bird and took off at a run up the trail, disappearing into the trees.

The crow flew over the trees, cawing out a victory celebration with each flap of his wings. The sound of the bird, still in pursuit of the running bear, faded into the mountain side and dissipated over the ridge.

What was that all about? Breathing a huge sigh of relief, I muttered a prayer of gratitude. I crawled halfway out of the water, retrieved the gun, checked it out for damage and secured it back into the holster on my belt. I took another deep breath and leaned heavily back into the moss covered soil, surrounding the pool.

Everything had happened fast. There hadn't been any time to process the events. My brain felt numb... I wondered if it really might be a dream.

I had just fallen off a cliff into a pool of water after shooting and killing a bear. My broken and useless hand had somehow became like new and the dead bear with his head blown off, had just got up and ran into the woods.

The WATER. It was the water. What else could it have been? I had fallen into a spring of anointed water and had been cured. Just like that. It was the kind of stuff people of Jesus would shout about. A true miracle. Sign of the second coming.

I had a thousand questions.

Somebody had to have some answers.

I thought of Uncle Paul. If anybody knew, he would.

I reached down and cupped my hand in the miracle water. Looking close, I saw the water had a golden tone of color and was as clear as the morning mist.

I sniffed it. There was something about the odor that was puzzling familiar. I sipped the water from my hand and smacked my lips. That taste. What was it?

Then I had it. Moonshine...

It had the aroma and taste similar to Uncle Paul's Tennessee Finest. Was the stream the root channel or maybe a tributary from Uncle Paul's water source for his moonshine? My mind became confused at what was happening. I couldn't think straight. The miracle water had something to do with... Moonshine? My thought process got stuck in a neutral gear. I was going to have to try and figure this out.

I had stumbled upon and found something. I knew that. What miracle had I uncovered? I wasn't sure. From a stream of water in Jarman Hollow, I had discovered a source of renewal in flesh and spirit? Why hadn't someone found this before? Someone else had to have experienced this mysterious stream of water. This was not the kind of stuff anybody would or could keep secret.

Water that heals and raises from the dead? This whole affair was taking on biblical overtures. Wow. A huge feeling of comfort came over me when the possibilities came rolling over and over around in my brain. I felt a rush of excitement.

I took several deep breaths and tried to calm down. My heart was racing.

First things first. I had to get my water container filled and get back to my Rover as fast as I could. I figured I had about forty more minutes of daylight and I didn't want to be stumbling around these trails in the dark. Plus, my friend the bear might decide to come back for Round Two.

I smacked my right hand with my left hand balled into a tight fist. Flexing my hand muscles, I admired the dexterity of the movement.

Shaking my head in disbelief, I kept saying to myself, 'Thank you, Lord... Thank you, Lord'. This miracle water had to have a supreme being behind it. With all my fiber, I knew it.

I felt the budge in my back pocket and remembered the flask I brought. The traditions of my ancestors came to mind and I felt I needed to show my gratitude immediately.

Removing the cap on the metal container, I filled it with the miracle water and held it up into the air. I said a toast and prayer of thanks and then took a long, deep drink of the cold water. It tasted sweet and refreshing. After drinking about half the water in the flask, I refilled it, put the cap on tightly and put it back in my pants pocket. I felt the acknowledgment of a higher power was in order. It made me feel good.

Grabbing the five gallon container beside me, in my excitement, I fumbled with the lid to get it off. Holding it underwater with both hands, it filled within a minute.

As it was filling, I took a look around and noticed there were drying spots of moss around the bank. The shoreline was getting larger which indicated the water level of the pool had dropped. I looked up to see the waterfall starting again. That must be how this thing works, I thought, the pool gets low and refills, a constant progression hidden by nature and reoccurring through the ages. I heard the water gushing out of the pool bed toward the overflow. In the center of the pool, the water swirled around in a slow circle.

My plan was to go back to the Rover and bring all the containers to refill them with the healing water. I had to share this with the world. I could carry two containers at a time and it shouldn't take too long.

I was surprised at how light the Five gallon container seemed after filling it with water. I felt invigorated and stronger than ever.

Occasionally, I could still hear the crow cawing in the distance on the other side of the ridge. 'Thank you, my brother,' I said sincerely. There was no telling what could have happened if the bird had not been there. I could not think of an earthly explanation why a crow would do that sort of thing. Another miracle, I thought.

I started up the trail with the five gallons of special cargo back to the highway.

I was surprised at how quick I made the hike, as I was at the Rover within minutes. I popped the hood and filled the cooled radiator with the special water. It only took a small portion of the container.

Closing and securing the hood, I walked to the back of the vehicle. I hurriedly unpacked two more containers from the back of the Rover. These transparent containers would normally have been filled with Paul's Tennessee Finest and headed back to Knoxville. Providence had dictated otherwise… now, I was going to fill them with something a lot more valuable.

After seeing the trail, I felt confident at moving at a faster speed. I was sure the bear had left for a different part of the mountain so I didn't really think about him again. Holding the plastic containers, I moved at a slow jog down the trail, stopping at the point overlooking the pool where the bear and I initially fell.

The silence in the forest was overwhelming.

No animals stirred. No birds flew. A stilled quietness surrounded the trees like the funeral silence at a locked up mortuary.

The waterfall was gone. It had disappeared completely. Not even a drip remained.

I stopped at the over-point of the cliff where I had fallen, and was shocked to see the pool of water down below, had shrunk to about half the size it was when I started back up to the Rover.

The slow, circular current in the center of the pool, had become whitewater as it sped up in speed, circling and sucking downward into a coned spiral… swirling like a small tornado. Like pulling the plug in the bathtub.

The pool was shrinking.
Fast.
The miracle stream was disappearing right before my eyes.

## **Chapter Three**
## **AMBUSH IN THE DARK**

My legs stopped working. The thought of the miracle water disappearing before the world could feel its benefits, hit me hard. I felt a sense of panic. What do I do? Whatever it was, I knew I had to move fast.

I had two empty containers with me. I had to try and save as much of the precious water as I could before it completely disappeared.

A sense of urgency made my brain click into high gear.

I had seventeen containers left in the rear of the Rover. I had to get them unstrapped and down to the pool as quickly as I could.

I threw the two empty containers in my hands, over the cliff and down to the exposed shoreline. I ran back up the trail to the Rover.

Within minutes I had the seventeen containers out of the Rover and strapped together to where I could drag them behind me. Coming back up the trail would be a whole different problem... right now, I needed to concentrate on getting the water into the containers. Afterwards, I'll worry about getting the filled containers back to the Rover.

Rushing back down the trail to the point above the pool of water, I threw the strapped containers over the cliff and to the moss covered shoreline below. I saw where the pool size had shrunk even further in the few minutes it had taken me to get to the Rover.

I continued running down the trail. Dodging most of the tree limbs and thorny bushes overlapping the tail, I hit and scrapped my arm again an Elm tree. The impact peeled my skin back and exposed brilliant red, blood vessels. I barely noticed the sting as I sped down to the pond.

Reaching the pond, I grabbed the stack of containers and pulled them into the pool's center of disappearing water. The plastic containers floated easily, plus the current was running in the direction I was going.

Undoing the caps on two containers, I held them under water infill they were full. Holding them completely under was difficult as the water level of the pool was dropping fast. There seemed to be a vacuum pulling the water downward and the pull of the current made it hard to hold the containers from being pulled from my hands and into the vortex at the center of the pool. I braced my feet into the rocky bottom of the pool and when both containers were full, I dragged them to the ever growing moss covered bank, which was now only ten feet from where I stood. Grabbing two more empty containers I struggled to get into position where I could put the containers under my body to fill them.

A stinging sensation made me glance down at the water running over my arm where I gouged the skin back, when I hit the tree as I ran down the trail. The abrasion had disappeared in a matter of seconds. No blood. The pain stopped. Healed. Again.

Straddling over the buoyant containers and holding them between my legs, seemed to be the easiest and fastest way to fill them with the precious water.

The water lever had dropped from my waist to my knees within minutes.

After filling the containers, I dragged them over to the dry land and put the caps on.

Four containers filled…

I only had four filled.

The water level dropped below my knees.

I grabbed two more plastic jugs, turned them on their sides and held them tightly against the rocks on the bottom. The rocks were now visible and I could see air bubbles escaping from crevices among the underwater stones.

The water level dropped to my ankles.

Air, in the two remaining containers I was holding, was released as the water level fell below the cap hole. I fell to my knees in the remaining kid size pool of water and used my hands to cup as much water into each of the plastic can's openings.

Then the water was gone.

With a gurgling sound that echoed off the walls of the cliff, the last remnants of healing fluid had gone from a clear golden pool, to nothing but a riverbed of rock on the side of a mountain.

I stood in the center of the crater where a pool of water would have been twelve feet over my head. Now, there was nothing but slippery pieces of granite and stone with a golden hue that changed to grey as the rocks dried.

The water in the two remaining plastic containers combined only equaled to about three gallons total.

The sound of the crow came from trees growing on the side of the cliff. I had not seen him fly in. He cawed several times and was silent. I did not see him in the branches. I assumed it was the same crow that had saved my life. Hearing the bird reminded me the bear could have doubled back. I patted the gun attached to my belt. If he pops up, I'll deal with him.

I had to move. And move fast. It was getting dark.

I checked each of the full containers and made sure the cap was on tightly and no leaks. Now, I had to get them back up the trail to the Rover. I looked around at the drying rocks where the pool had once been. Who is going to believe this?... I thought.

They will when they see what this water does, I countered in my head, as I picked up two full containers and struggled up the trail to the Rover.

The sun had disappeared behind the mountains when I finished packing the water in the back of the Rover. I loaded the full containers last after packing the empty ones in the middle seat area. I strapped them down to make them as secure as possible.

I got in the vehicle, adjusted the seat and took a deep breath. I was wore out on the outside. The containers seemed to get heavier with every step I took uphill. It had been a long day. One I would never forget.

On the inside, I felt the warmness a person feels when doing something good for other people. The miracle water had been a gift from God. I was certain of it.

An uncomfortable budge in my hip reminded me of Uncle Paul's present I had in my back pocket. Reaching back and pulling the flask out, I slipped it into the side door panel of the Rover. Covering it with a handful of napkins to keep it a hidden surprise, I couldn't wait to give it to him.

He was not going to believe the story I was going to tell him. I hoped he would have the answers for all the questions I had.

Starting the engine on the Rover, I was happy to see all the warning lights were off. The motor hummed like it was supposed too.

There was no moon in the sky so the night was totally black. I turned on the headlights, pulled out onto the highway and sped a lot faster than I should have... considering the curves in the road.

The two miles to the turn off to Uncle Paul's road went by quickly.

I went through a tunnel and made a sharp blind turn to the break in the roadside, leading to the entrance of the logging road.

I turned the Rover off the road with my bright lights on and stopped immediately once I was off the road. This spot on the trip was one of the few where my phone would still receive emails and voice messages. I gave a quick glance at the messages I had missed.

I saw I had a message from my sister in Florida. She was with my Mother who was recuperating from cancer surgery. I immediately clicked the button to listen.

It was bad news.

The message was an urgent plea to come to Florida at once. My Mother had taken a turn for the worse. My sister had to take her to the ER because of hemorrhaging. Her Doctors had given her the ok to go to Florida with just a few warnings and exceptions. Her medications and a light exercise program had been prescribed. Lots of sunshine, was my sister's cure and was included in their plans. She was looking good, getting around well and was excited about life. But, something had gone wrong. She was in trouble.

Devastated after listening to the message, it didn't look good.

Come as fast as you can… my sister kept saying in the message.

My chest was tight with fear but I also felt hope.

I had the cure.

I had the cure in the back of my Rover. It was either God, in his all knowing presence, or something from another planet that had given me the anointing water. And the water would save my Mom. I knew it. The whole series of events in the past twelve hours had brought me to this moment. My Mother's fate was in my hands. This whole thing was something from a terrestrial or heavenly plan.

Call it fate. Call it providence. Call it whatever you want, but I knew what I had to do.

I had to get to Florida.

The trees, along the ruts in the so-called road, threw huge shadows that jiggled and bounced in the headlights with every motion of the Rover's wheels. My Mother would live. I would see to that. I had seen the miracles with the bear and my arm. I knew the healing water would save her.

There was a wide spot amongst the trees ahead to turn around and I could get back on the highway.

Uncle Paul, the moonshine, the questions about healing water…everything was going to have to wait. I slowed down to cross a stream that ran across the road, forming a wide, clear area in the trees. Putting the Rover in reverse, I backed up. My heart pounded with urgency to get back on the main road and I said a prayer for my Mom.

Suddenly, I slammed on the brakes and covered my face with my arms as the whole world lit up and sirens split the night's quietness.

Blinded by intense lights shining into the interior of the stopped Rover, I tried to peer out of half closed eyes at what was happening.

Brilliant red, blue and white lights were twirling and spinning amongst the forest, casting millions of moving shadows and disorienting me. Sirens blasted into my ears and I was aware of people surrounding the Rover, moving into position around me.

The sirens stopped.

A loud-speakered voice reverberated from the darkness beyond the trees.

Dreaded words nobody in this part of the country ever wants to hear.

"Federal agents…Keep your hands where we can see them!"

## Chapter Four
## Uncle Paul

An authoritative, high feminine voice broke through the darkness behind the haze of lights and the sound of numerous people moving through the trees.

"Step out of the car with your hands out to your sides, sir...NOW!"

I hesitated. Time was short. My Mom. I had to get to my Mom.

I needed to express the urgency to whoever controlled the lights and sirens.

"Yes, Officer," I said, to the female agent. I opened the door and stuck one foot out. "No problem, but I need to get back on the road. I was just turning around... my Mother is sick and ..."

The federal agent took a step back.

"I said NOW, Mister', she snapped

Two good sized men stepped in and grabbed my arms. Twisting my body to the side, they patted me down and then laid me over the hood, cuffing my hands behind my back.

My emotions were exploding inside of me. I knew if I fought them it would only make it worse. On the other hand, I had to get free. Each minute was precious.

"Officer, what is this all about?", I pleaded. This couldn't be happening. Not now.

The two male agents turned me around and walked me to the back door of a waiting black SUV.

Walking behind us, the high voice Agent said, "You are being detained under investigation for violation of 26 United States Code, Section 506." She continued with the Miranda warning as the two men pushed me into the backseat and closed the door.

26 United States Code, Section 506?

Moonshining? They were busting me for moonshining!

It was like a bad dream. I couldn't take my eyes off my Rover and had to bend my neck sideways to keep it in view. The precious water I had been able to save, was in that car. I saw a dark figure get in and maneuver the Rover into the procession of lighted vehicles moving slowing up the bumpy road.

My heart was pounding with fear and anger. I feared for my Mother's life and I was angry enough to take someone's life… if the delay continued.

I had to escape.

I scanned the backseat of the SUV, the agent's body posture and their position to the door handles. I tested the handcuffs behind my back. None of the possible options of escape that ran through my head seem to have any chance of success.

I would have to wait my chance… then take it. No hesitation.

It took about four minutes to complete the trip up the logging road to Uncle Paul's mountain cabin. It was a bumpy ride over the ruts and deep holes in the dirt road.

When the caravan finally stopped, I could see by the lights on the porch that Uncle Paul wasn't there. It's the little things, but I know there's a light on the back porch he leaves on when he's on a trip. When he's there, he turns it off. He's been doing that for twenty years. The light was on so he probably wasn't there, and hadn't been there. I felt relief. I didn't want him caught up in this.

Most of the activity of the agents was at the large metal barn behind the small A-Frame cabin positioned in front of a large, turnaround area. Lights were being set up around the perimeter of the buildings. People were carrying armloads of material from the huge double doors and forming a pile in the turnaround driveway up from the cabin and barn. I watched as my Rover pulled away from the procession of vehicles and parked close to the barn. I lost sight of the Rover when two other vehicles pulled in front of it.

I wondered where Uncle Paul was and how I could warn him. I had to escape now. I could kill a couple of these people and get away. I didn't want to, but when it came to family, I would do it without a second thought. I was capable of doing that. I could turn right and wrong morals, off and on like a light switch. In the Army, I had been stationed at Fort Campbell with an outfit that was trained to do unspeakable and totally uncivilized things in combat. Having said that, war could be declared within minutes. And when it comes to family... blood runs deep when you're from the mountains.

Each minute was an eternity to me in getting to my Mother's side. Uncle Paul had to know about my Mother's conditions. I must have been out of cell phone range when my sister contacted the both of us. My Mother was his baby sister. He would move heaven and earth for her. I felt some comfort thinking he might have flown down to be with my Mom.

Stereotypes of moonshiners have been portrayed in books, television and movies through the years. That image has become synonymous with slow, thinking, tobacco chewing, lazy hillbillies... just ignorant hicks living in mountain squalor.

Uncle Paul would laugh whenever that stereotype popped up anywhere.

Uncle Paul was not that kind of moonshiner.

As a child growing up in the mountains, his mind

was an insatiable vacuum for knowledge. With little or no electricity, there were no lights or conveniences, certainly no television. To entertain his active brain, he would devour any kind of book available. An hour and a half hour drive down the mountain to the County Library once a month, would reward him with a paper sack full of books. Or he would borrow books from friends who might have a more extensive and uncensored collection.

He worshiped his father, James Paul Stonewall and as soon as he could walk, they spent a great deal of time together hunting, fishing and making Jarman Hollow moonshine. Uncle Paul would sit for hours listening to JP Stonewall tell stories from the generations that his Daddy and Momma had passed on to him. If Uncle Paul wasn't reading, he probably was making moonshine, listening to stories.

After graduating high school, Uncle Paul enrolled at the University of Tennessee, going to school in the summer and fall months and spending the rest of the time making the finest moonshine whiskey this side of the Mississippi.

By the time he was thirty, Uncle Paul had earned two college degrees, spoke three languages and could curse in six, had a 6th degree black belt in Isshin-Ryū Karate and could tear a fiddle up with bona fide bluegrass tunes or make you cry with a haunting Brahm's lullaby... depending on requests and how much he's had to drink. Uncle Paul was a tough old bird and the only flaw I knew he had, was he couldn't sing a lick, although he loved to attempt it. In Tennessee, everybody knows that's a crime... not to be able to sing, but we forgave him because of the enthrusiasim and confidence he put into every horrible rendition of Rocky Top he would belt out. He could always bring down the house at Open Mics on whatever continent he might be.

I've seen him numerous times in places all over the world from Tokyo to London to Moscow, rubbing elbows with families and customers in high-dollar whiskey circles, who thought they knew him well enough, to ask why he kept on making moonshine when he was obviously well-educated and successful. He would always give the same reply... and end with the same poem.

"Passion, my friends," he would say... "and tradition. Passion, instilled in me with lessons from my father and his father, and their traditions, handed down through generations of mountain people. My forefathers moved from the highlands of Scotland to the mountains of Tennessee. They married into my grandmother's people, the Cherokee and passed our stores through time.

> The blood of the Scots and Cherokee,
> and moonshine whiskey run through me...
> so buy a jug, or I say no more,
> life stories aren't for free,
> you know?"

Then with a big southern laugh, he would hold up a gallon jug of Paul's Tennessee's Finest in the face of the questioner, and then sell it, in the early days, for five thousand dollars. (Now if you can find a gallon of Paul's Tennessee Finest for fifteen thousand...consider yourself lucky.)

Afterwards, he would enthrall the buyer's imaginations and close the deal with Scottish tales of mountain lore or spirit tales of the forest lived by Cherokee warriors. He was a magnificent storyteller with P.T. Barnum's imagination and bullshit ability, and Davy Crockett's character and persona. Everyone who met Uncle Paul considered, or wanted him as, a close personal friend afterwards. He was just that way. People fell in love with him.

    I loved him.

    Today is his birthday.

    I brought him a present. That was the initial reason I had planned on being here today. It was to pick up a load of Paul's Tennessee Finest and to celebrate Uncle Paul's birthday... only not under these circumstances.

    The number of working people in the lighted area away from the barn, was growing. I estimated about fifteen to twenty people milling around the property. Lights were continuing to be set up to illuminate the driveway, cabin and barn. I kept craning my head in various positions to see through the windows and see what was going on around me. The lights and Agents moving outside the SUV made it difficult to focus on anything specific.

    I did see the constructed pile had grown larger with different parts added from the numerous stills Uncle Paul had in operation inside the huge barn. The agents were dismantling them bit by bit and adding them to the stack. Wooden barrels and plastic containers were being thrown in amongst bags of sugar and yeast.

    The agents standing outside SUV guarding me, moved away a couple of feet to talk on their radios. Every Agent it seemed in the area had some type of radio they were constantly relaying different information to whoever was in charge. A lot of TEN FOURS and COPY THAT... from what I could hear through the vented windows. The ATF Task Force had expected my Uncle Paul to be there and wasn't sure what to do or what the procedure should be since he wasn't there...

    Suddenly, there was a huge commotion on the property located above the cabin and behind the barn, as the whole area was lit up by directional lights pointing to its center, revealing a huge, squared clear area. A brighter series of bank lights came on immediately afterwards, showing a twenty yard piece of pavement, with painted markings and flashing red lights, surrounding the edges of the pad.

In Jarman Hollow, in the interior of the Smokey Mountains, Uncle Paul had added a convenience to his property that surprises most first time vistitors.

A heliport.

I smiled at the confusion of the Agents as they scurried around investigating the source of the lights.

I knew all about the lights.

My Uncle Paul has two college degrees. One is in Computer Programing… the other Electrical Engineering. He took great pride in rigging up the remote system for the landing lights on his heliport so he could control them from the air whenever he flew in. I had helped him do all the grunt work.

I heard the sound of a helicopter in the distance.

I let out a long sigh. Relief and hope… all in one expression.

Chop. Chop. Chop. The sound of the helicopter blades got closer.

Uncle Paul was coming.

# Chapter Five
# Blood In The Water

The silver and blue Airbus H135 swooped down into the clearing and hovered a couple of hundred feet above the heliport. The graphic of a silhouetted black bear against a white mountain range and topped with a bold PJS, were incorporated into the design of the sleek helicopter. I knew on the H135, the night vision imaging system was standard equipment and with the additional video and camera systems Uncle Paul had installed on board and hooked into his security systems at the cabin, he had been up to speed of everything going on with an up close and personal view.

The rotors slowed as the craft landed in the middle of the pad. Once they stopped, both side doors opened and two men stepped down.

All the Agents had immediately ran toward the heliport and surrounded the helicopter with weapons drawn.

With everything lit up, my vantage point in the back seat of the SUV couldn't have been better. I immediately recognized the pilot as Uncle Paul, and the passenger was Kevin Gene 'Senator' Yona, a full blooded Cherokee Indian and the family lawyer.

Uncle Paul and Kevin Gene (or 'Senator,' as most of the people in Swain and Jackson Counties called him) grew up in the mountains together and both had gone to school at the University of Tennessee. The bond between the two men ran deep, witnessed by stories I had heard countless times on hunting and fishing trips.

The two men stopped and Kevin Gene waved a handful of papers in the air and with his other hand in a clenched fist, he punched the air for emphasis as he was yelling at the Agents.

I could not hear or understand what the lawyer was saying. He was animated and frantically waving his arms and papers around. Uncle Paul would interrupt him periodically, and they both would angrily point at the parked SUV I was in.

The Agents kept pointing their guns at the two men. The tension grew with the shouting between the two groups. Finally what must have been a consensus, and at Kevin Gene's insistence, the Agents lowered their weapons and approached the two men for a more peaceful parlay.

I saw one Agent snatch the papers from Kevin Gene and appeared to be examining them. The two men looked to be having a heated discussion.

Uncle Paul suddenly threw up his hands, motioned to a female Agent in the group to follow him and started walking toward the SUV, where I was still handcuffed in the backseat.

Each Agent received a challenging glare as they moved aside to let him pass. With his head back, shoulder squared walk, everyone in the group knew Paul J. Stonewall was not to be messed with. The tall man with the bald head and chest length beard, had the look of a WWE wrestler parading to the ring ready to do battle. The female Agent he had motioned, nodded and fell in walking behind him, trying to lengthen her stride to keep up with the larger man.

They walked directly to the SUV and Uncle Paul stood to the side as the Agent opened the door, helped me out and stood there, holding on to me by the handcuffs. She kept looking back at the group of Agents still conversing with Kevin Gene back at the heliport. One of the Agents stepped out and waved to her, nodding his head up and down.

She immediately unlocked the handcuffs and then muttered a 'Kamala Salad' about it was all a mistake, and on behalf of the Agency she would like to extend a sincere apology. She then turned and walked back up to the group without further explanation, how de do or kiss my ass.

My uncle's eyes had met as soon as the Agent had opened the SUV to let me out. His look said it all without saying a word. Don't speak... wait. Just wait. He stood by and didn't speak until the Agent left.

"Come on," he said, grabbing my arm, he guided me to the porch steps up to the cabin. We walked to the door and I stood to the side as he unlocked it. Stepping over the threshold, he flipped several switches beside the doorframe.

Turning to me, he grabbed both my shoulders and looked me up and down. He was tall and I had to bend my neck back to be able meet his gaze.

"You ok, boy?", he said, eyes locked into mine. The look was almost a stare. He could spot any emotion or lie in a millisecond with that look. That was one of the reasons why I never played Poker with him. He continued with a worried tone in his voice, "Have you heard? Your Mom is in a bad way. I came to find you. We've got to go as soon as we get this mess settled."

"Uncle Paul, look," I said and held up my left hand in front of him, "see this. My hand...look". I flexed my fingers and made a fist several times.

Uncle Paul's eyes widen and he gasped in surprise as he examined my hand and arm. He had just seen my hand in the Emergency Room when my Mom called him to go check on me. He had seen the skinned and mangled bones, ligaments and tendons assembled into something that resembled a claw more than a hand. He had been concerned I would ever have full use of the hand after the accident. Now, he was looking at a hand without blemish.

A perfect hand in every detail.

I guided him to the couch in the room and motioned for him to sit down. Looking bewildered, he sat down and held my hand to hold and examine. Rubbing the skin on my fingers, he slowly turned them to expose my palm and wrist.

I said, "Time is short, I know we've got to go…and I want to know what's going on with these Federal people, but right now, you've GOT to listen to my story. There's a chance for Mom. You gotta believe me."

Uncle Paul sensed my urgency. "Go ahead, son, say your piece," he said, "Kevin Gene will take care of those people outside."

I told him the story.

All of it.

From the time I pulled over needing water, to killing the bear, to my hand being miraculously being healed, to the dead bear coming alive to attack again, how the mysterious crow saved me, what I did when I realized the power of the miracle water, and the sudden disappearance of the pool into the mountain side.

With each part of the incredible story my Uncle would inch closer to me in total amazement.

After I finished my story, Uncle Paul sit back into the couch and let out a long, deep breath. He had a thoughtful look on his face.

"You found the **Healing Stream**," said Kevin Gene Yona. He had come in the side door behind me. Kevin Gene moved quietly everywhere, after all he was an Indian. His face was still red from his ferocious argument with the Agents. I had been so engrossed in telling Uncle Paul what had happened I didn't notice him coming into the cabin

"You found the **Healing Steam**," he

repeated,"don't you think so, Gusdi? He directed the question to Uncle Paul calling him 'Cousin' in Cherokee. "Isn't that the tale, Grandma Gooki use to tell us and said it was a Cherokee legend of the old people?"

Lights from the Agent's vehicles and loud sounds of engines revving, cut through the windows of the cabin as the caravan outside cranked up and moved down the driveway, away from the cabin. The ATF people were leaving. It looked like a parade as the Federal Agents inched around holes and sporadic ditches in the dirt road.

The movement of the officers was just background and white noise to me. I zoned in immediately at what I had just heard. I turned to Kevin Gene quickly. "**The Healing Steam**? You've heard about it?"

"You said there was a bear and crow near the water…I think that's what Grandma Gooki said. You remember?" he asked, motioning to Uncle Paul. He walked over and sit down in a lounge chair. Grandma Gooki was a Cherokee elder who had watched after Uncle Paul and Kevin Gene when they were young, barefooted and running the woods. She had help raise dozens of kids around Jarman Hollow.

"**The Healing Steam**," Uncle Paul said slowly, "you found the **Healing Stream**…Grandma Gooki said the stream would appear and disappear without warning. Supposedly, the magical stream was formed from the tears of ancient Mother's who had lost their children and cried themselves to death. The story goes, blood in the stream releases it's magic and sickness, disease and injury are vanquished. Along with the healing power of the water, the miracles travel with those who have quenched their thirst straight from the stream."

"That's right," Kevin Gene interjected,"The miracles travel with those who drank from the stream. Did you drink any of this water?

I stood up and held my hand in front of my Uncle's and Kevin Gene's face. "I not only drank it, I have almost twenty gallons out in my Rover. Come on, we've got to go. I can tell you more on the way. Mom needs us. Uncle Paul, I assume you can fly us down on the 135? Are we done with those buttheads trying to arrest me for moonshining?"

I turned to walk out the front door of the cabin. I stopped and hesitated, waiting for replies to my questions.

I still had a thousand questions about the healing stream. But, time was running out. We could talk in the helicopter once we got in the air.

Kevin Gene hurriedly got up from the lounge chair, grabbed some papers and jammed them into a briefcase by his side.

"Federal people won't bother you anymore, Paul," said Kevin Gene as he put a hand on his old friends shoulder. He continued, "Seems like they didn't realize Jarman Hollow is on reservation land of the Eastern Band of Cherokee. They have no jurisdiction here. I informed them of possible civil litigation in the future. Stupid bastards. Keep making your whisky, Paul. Good thing we got here when we did, they were getting ready to put a torch to your stills. There were going to destroy everything."

Uncle Paul moved to the door, "Thanks Kev, let's get in the air. Ruthie needs us."

My heart froze when I heard what Kevin Gene had just said.

They were going to destroy everything.

"No," I said in disbelief. No, they wouldn't damage the water containers. Would they?

I ran from the cabin and up to the side of the barn where the Agents had left my Rover. I heard my Uncle and Kevin hurrying behind me. There were no other vehicles in the driveway and the area was lit up by the spotlights on the corners of the metal building.

The four doors on the Rover were wide open. The back gate was wide open. The interior lights showed the vehicle was empty.

Nothing. The plastic containers were gone.

I ran up beside the car, wringing my hands and holding my head, pacing back and forth. The coldness around my heart turned black with thoughts of revenge at the Federal Agents. All the containers were lying on their side beside the barn.

All were empty.

The miracle water was gone.

## Chapter Six
## When Mothers Wept

There was an explosion in my brain as I processed what had just happened. The miracle water I had worked so hard to save had been poured out because some bureaucrat thought it would be used to make moonshine? ... because of a foul up in paperwork?...these Federal idiots didn't know to read a map?

I was pacing back and forth when Uncle Paul and Kevin Gene got to the car. My belief the miracle water would save my Mother had given me hope. I had seen what the mountain stream had done. My hand had been healed and a dead bear was prowling the mountainsides. I was having trouble thinking or speaking. Keeping my balance while trying to walk was getting more difficult. I was overcome with emotion.

The water was gone. Just like that.

"What is it, boy?" Uncle Paul asked, walking up behind me.

I fought to get the words out of my mouth.

"It's gone, Uncle Paul," I said,"those bastards poured it out. The water, its gone. Gone."

I shook my head back and forth in denial of what had happened.

"The water's gone?" asked Kevin Gene credulously, walking around the car and kicking an empty container, "No, they didn't do that, did they?"

The sound of a crow's caw came from top of the barn. We instinctively looked up to see the bird flying around in the spotlight and landing on the roof. All three of us gave each other a quick questioning look.

A crow? In the dark?

Now…?

I tried to control my breathing.

A rush of mental images played in my head. I had come into the mountains to stock up on Paul's Tennessee's Finest moonshine, had car trouble, killed a bear, fell into a magical pool, my injured hand was healed, the dead bear came alive and attacked me again when this crow intervened and probably saved me…and now…

Now, a crow, my gut told me it was the same crow that saved me from the bear, shows up when Federal Agents have destroyed what could have been the only hope in saving my Mother's life. The turn of events were spinning in my head.

In most of the stories I heard in my childhood, the crow had represented a symbol of communication between worlds… traveling through different dimensions before the recording of time. Where omens and spells among the Cherokee affected every phase of their lives.

Maybe the crow appearing, was a message.

Wait! Another thought stopped me from moving. I came to the mountains to stock up, but, ALSO to celebrate

Uncle's Paul's birthday.

His present! The flask! It still had water in it when I stashed it in the Rover.

I felt hope. There might still be a chance.

Had the Agents's gotten to it too?

I rushed over to the driver's door and looked under the clump of napkins I had jammed over the flask to conceal it in the door panel.

The napkins were the there. I threw them into the front seat.

The flask was there. I picked it up and shook it vigorously.

Nothing.

The flask was empty.

The Agents had emptied the flask along with the containers.

The crow started the same tempo, cawing that had become so annoying at the pool. I took it as a sign this saga was not over. I had seen what the crow could do when it had attacked the bear.

I'm a grown man. A combat veteran. I have seen things, and done thing in war that most human beings could not imagine. Crying is not something I have done much in my life. I'm 6 foot and four inches and hold my weight pretty good, so crying in my peer group was usually not accepted to well.

I only remember crying real tears in public twice. Once, when I was fourteen and had to put my horse down. She was special and I remember standing in the stall crying like a baby. But, she was in pain… and I had to let her go.

I cried real tears then.

The last time I cried, I was holding my Mother when she told me she had cancer. It was a cry with her, but I had such an immense feeling of failure as her protector, and a son's feelings of helplessness in not knowing what to do to help her, I cried for myself too. Call it crazy, call it whatever you want, I felt failure. Somehow, I felt should have protected her from that damn disease.

That's what Fathers and Sons do. We protect the ones we love. Anyway. Anyhow. That's our job. The pain we see in others becomes our pain. Even though logic and reason told me there wasn't anything I could have done to prevent her disease, I still cried.

And now, I have failed her again.

I should have protected the water much better… it was destiny for me to discover the pool. I had a chance to save her.

The rush of emotion made me choke as I fell to my knees. The pain of having a miracle in my grasp…virtually in my hands, and then losing it…just like that.

Suddenly my eyes overflowed with tears of grief. I felt a tightness in my chest that made it difficult to breathe. Sobbing uncontrollably, the thought of the death of my Mother filled me with immense sorrow.

Uncle Paul came and put his hand on my shoulder.

"Come on, son, there was nothing you can do," he said in a consoling and surprisingly gentle tone.

I was bent over covering my face in unspeakable grief. The miracle water was gone… forever. The tears kept flowing and I wanted whatever privacy possible to veil my emotions. Even if it was just a curtain of flesh I made with my hands, I wanted to hide my face from the men.

Kevin Gene came to my side and reached down to help me up.

When he grabbed my arms to pull my hands from my face, he quickly took a step back

"Mother of Jesus," he exclaimed, "Gusdi, look!" pointing at my face. Uncle Paul stepped back so the barn lights could shine on my face.

The tears running down my face were large and

luminous. The golden hue of the droplets, falling off my chin, changed to a brilliant hue of sky blue when they hit the ground to form small puddles. Like rainbows in bubbles, an image of celestial and cosmic birth, rarely seen by mortal humans.

My wet, tear covered, hands shown with a golden florescence, glittering in the spotlights from the barn.

The two other men took another step back.

"The tears from the ancient Mothers?" said Uncle Paul, looking to Kevin Gene and taking a deep breath, he continued, " the Healing Stream?" He had a reverent tone to his question.

They were witnessing something not from this world. Something ancient, born in words and omens spoken after a Mother's heartbreak from losing a child. The countless tears cried at bedsides and gravesides. The tears from farewells with the final and last kiss.

Those tears

Kevin Gene's tone was somber. He spoke as a Cherokee Indian who honored the stories from his ancestors. These stories had been Kevin Gene's and Paul Stonewall's history lessons as children.

"Cherokee legend tells about the sorrows of our Mothers in the days of the Early Ones. Those sorrows shaped changed and became powerful enough to help those in pain, both in spirit and in body. All the Mother's tears, created in severe pain from their loss, came together to form a gift of a 'magical stream' of tears. If you can imagine, a stream that appears and disappears with the ages. A stream of life for those who bathe in the waters are healed, and those who drink of the waters, CAN THEN take miracles to all tribes, to the masses… remember Gusdi? Remember what Grandma Gooki said? They take miracles to the masses…" His voice trailed off as the significance of his statement was realized by all the men.

The crow cawed several times and took flight in a southward direction. It was almost morning.

"Come on, boy. Let's go," said Uncle Paul, picking me up and guiding me toward the helicopter, "Ruthies' waiting... you Mother needs you." He motioned to Kevin Gene to help him guide me. There was no doubt the two men knew I was the miracle in the legend.

I touched the wetness on my cheeks and gently rubbed the golden liquid between my palms. The realization of the power I now carried was humbling and although, thankful, I couldn't understand why I was chosen. Tears welled up in my eyes, just thinking about seeing my Mother in a couple of hours.

As foretold, I will take miracles to the masses.

The miracle of tears... from the Healing Stream.

As we boarded the helicopter, the morning sun peeked over the mountaintops as another day was being born. Somewhere deep in the Smokey Mountains in a quiet valley covered with the greens and browns of foliage, a black bear stops and sniffs the ground where a small trickle of water is gurgling out of a crack in a rocky bank. The bear walks away as droplets of golden water start to form a small pool...

**The Healing Stream**.

**The end**

# Fiver Dean

## Chapter One
# Dying In Public

The intense heat caused Fiver to squeeze his eyes shut.

As bright light fought to enter the crevices of his eyelashes, a disturbing thought came to him.

I never thought I would die like this. Not in an oven...

He had wondered how his last day would be. Would specific scenes of his life be highlighted, and plastered on neon billboards? Would they spin around in his head? There was something intriguing about moving on to the unknown. It would certainly release him from the pain he was in.

Fiver Dean relaxed his shoulders and decided to accept his fate without any whimper. Die like a man, he thought, Pop would be proud.

He started to feel his chest constrict. It was getting hard to breathe.

The heat was becoming unbearable.

He thought about his sister.

He had another thought.

Were all the faucets in the hotel room closed tight? The Belmond Hotel Splendido would not like it if someone died at their hotel, and left the faucets on to boot.

He was conscious enough to realize, he was having strange thoughts for someone dying in an oven.

Must be thinking of Paris and George, or something... that's it! Fiver suddenly realized the origin of the thought.

Joyce, or 'George' as he called his younger sister,

had gone off for three months one time, and left her bathtub faucet dripping in her Paris apartment. She returned to a flood and unhappy French neighbors, who didn't appreciate the hole in their ceiling. The middle age husband didn't have a lot to say directly to Joyce about the incident. He had previously trapped her in the building elevator when she was returning home late one night. The balding, married man had made an improper move toward the long hair beauty, and had ended up with a broken thumb and a black eye. Joyce apologized profusely for the leak to his long suffering, wife, and took care of all the damages to both apartments. Everybody ended up happy. Especially the husband, when Joyce moved to Greece two months later.

Fiver felt the sweat run from his brow down to his shoulder. It was fitting he would think about his younger sister as he was dying. He and she were closer to each other than the other kids in their family. There was only a year difference in age between them.

He would miss George. She would not take his death well.

Fiver forced air down into his lungs to breathe.

The heat was killing him.

Fiver was the youngest boy amongst six children. His father, Axel, had a great sense of humor when it came to naming his children. Fiver's older siblings, sister Una, brothers Dual, Trey and Quad, took after their Mother, Dorothy, with fair complexions, red hair and quiet dispositions.

Fiver and his younger sister, Joyce had dark hair, were dark complexioned, and had charismatic, outgoing personalities. They never met a stranger anywhere they went. 'The Duo of Doom', as their older siblings use to call them, brought fun and laughter to whatever the event or occasion might be. Fiver and his younger sister, were extremely clever, when it came to pranks and practical jokes on the older children. As they grew older, they excelled in school and were offered scholarships to colleges and universities all over the world.

Joyce's name wasn't chosen the normal way Axel Dean had named his other five children. Fiver had learned from his Mother, when Joyce was born, their father was away as a guest of the Tennessee penal system. Axel Dean was at one time, one of the most prolific forgers in the lower southeastern states. He had, on one occasion, been lax in judgement in trusting the wrong person and it hadn't ended well. A message he would later preach and harp about constantly to his children on a daily basis. Know who you are dealing with, he would say.

When Joyce was born, Dorothy Dean, chose her name, while her husband was serving his time. Axel claimed he didn't even know his wife was pregnant, but thanked the Lord for the addition to his family anyhow. Upon his release, Axel had made a big deal about Joyce's name and proclaimed to the world the new baby would be nicknamed, 'Seis'. It sounded like he was calling her 'Sis', due to his refined southern drawl.

Fiver's own personal nickname for her, was 'George', because when he was a toddler he could not pronounce 'Joyce', and it came out sounding like George. So, it stuck.

Joyce 'George' Dean was a small framed, cute little girl, who worshiped the ground Fiver walked on. She would take Fiver's side immediately if there was any argument that couldn't be settled peacefully amongst the older siblings or the neighborhood kids. Fiver could take care of himself, but during the few times he was outnumbered by two or three adversaries, Joyce would protect his back and charge into the fray, screaming a ferocious battle cry. She was a whirlwind of fists and kicks that always evened the odds. None of the other boys, who were involved in those scrapes, wanted to deal with the little female hellion. She was as protective of Fiver as a mother lion.

Must be thinking about George and her Paris apartment. The thought repeated in his head.

Fiver laughed out loud at the memory, but immediately felt loneliness and sadness at the thought of not seeing his sister again. They had come a long way together. From a poor farm in Middle Tennessee, Fiver and George had used education and travel as the way to seek a different life. Fiver had left home, gone to Europe to find himself, and ended up joining the French Foreign Legion. After a tour in the Middle East, the seasoned soldier, enrolled into the University of Cambridge, in England.

George had graduated from the University of Chicago with an Art Degree, and moved to Paris to be closer to a more art driven culture. It was a lot of hard work and sacrifices for both of them. They made time to see each other on a regular basis, despite the distance and their hectic schedules. Ironically, it was while visiting George, at the University of Chicago, Fiver became interested in art... in a matter of speaking.

The heat had become unbearable.

This is it. He thought.

That was my last breath.

"Are you ready to do it or is it going to take more heat to change your stubborn mind? Are you going in or just lay over there and ignore me?"

The voice came from the darkness he had imposed on himself. It was a pleasant voice with an Italian accent.

Sweet. Soothing. Dangerous.

He cracked his right eye and turned his head to the side.

Uh-oh. Big mistake.

Before his right pupil immediately shutdown, from the blinding sunlight, the image of a beautiful woman in a red bikini, was burnt onto his retina.

Fiver had dozed off for a couple of minutes, by the noisy, Belmond Hotel Splendido pool, and wow… what kind of dream was that?

Dangerous thing to do in this heat. Drinking margaritas for lunch, on an empty stomach. Uh-oh…no, he was a grown man. He knew better than that. Sunburn is no fun. Dying in an oven? Really?

His eyes were taking a few seconds to adjust. The blurry, colorful, shapes in his retina started to evolve into the defined images of soft curves, blonde hair and a wicked grin., His eyes were adapting quickly, but the bright light was still uncomfortable for the moment. He put his arm above his face to block out the Italian sun.

'If you insist, let's do it," he said, with a hint of southern USA, creeping into his vowels. It was one of the things about Fiver that had endeared him to the hotel staff, restaurant employees and bartenders of the Belmond Hotel Splendido. The way he spoke Italian was incredible. His smooth, southern draw, spoken to the Italian rhythm, would make all the female employees start to tingle, and then try to engage him in a conversation. The fact, Fiver was one heck of a tipper also, didn't bother them either.

"Go on," she said, 'I just want to dab my face and admire your backside"

The tanned woman, with her long blonde hair, wrapped into a bun on her head, slowly eased back into her lounge chair, crossed one leg gracefully over the other, and picked up a small facecloth.

"Go on", she said again, "I'll be right behind you."

Fiver, threw a mock frown at one of Europe's most elegant, and most discreet, criminals. Bianca Pericoloso was the art fence to go to, for that specially desired painting. Bianca only dealt in six figure deals. Don't waste her time for less.

Bianca Pericoloso, and Fiver, had had done business with each other for three years. When the time called for it, Fiver would contact Bianca for her services. They were now lounging by the pool, celebrating the amount of money both would be making that evening in a mutual business transaction.

"Bianca, my sweet, you are a dirty young vixen and the Pope is going to send you straight to hell when you die," Fiver said.

The distinct Welsh, Sean Connery, accent, from the tall man lying in the deck chair, was crisp and musical ,when he spoke to the young woman beside him.

Fiver had many talents. Speaking four languages made it easy for him to impersonate many foreign accents, when the occasion or job, called for it.

Bianca Pericoloo, pushed strands of blond hair from the woven bun on her head away from her violet, blue eyes.

She smiled. Only her mouth smiled. Her eyes didn't.

She had striking eyes, separate from her beauty. Hypnotic. Piercing. When Bianca would blink…her eyes always seem to slow in closing, and then remained shut for a second. For that brief moment, sweet innocence would capture her face and frame it in aura of loveliness… and then…her eyes would reopen. Her looks would change. A coldness would return to her features. But… she was still a beautiful woman.

"If they have asini like yours, I'm ready to go now," Bianca coyly said, with that killer grin again. Her eyes flashed toward him, wanting appreciation for her joke.

Fiver, fully awake, looked over at the tanned curves of Bianca's skin, held together by her red bikini, and forgot all about the way her eyes looked.

He chuckled, swung his long legs from his deck chair and stood up.

Every woman, and some men, in the pool area of the Belmond Hotel Splendido in Portofino, Italy, as if one person, turned their heads and eyes toward him.

Fiver Dean was a handsome man. Movie handsome. Walking down the street, bump into a street light, handsome. He did not go anywhere people did not immediately notice him. His dark hair, tall frame, and chiseled looks, were like a coastal lighthouse, with an 'All You Can Eat' Buffet, Restaurant, below the flashing light, throwing out a welcome to any storm tossed ship, packed full of hungry, modern, starving women. It could get crazy if you hung around him.

He had an amazing knowledge on a great deal of subjects, and never had a problem carrying on a conversation with anyone, regardless of their station in life. From busboys to business leaders, maids to models, Fiver Dean was comfortable in everyone's company. They liked him instantly.

Fiver took the towel off his mid section and stood up.

A collective sigh, rose in the throats of the poolside women, watching him.

When you are one of the most professionally recognized, Art Dealers in France, and one of the most sought after art thieves in the world… Fiver had to admit…

it hadn't been all brains that had opened doors for him. Mother Nature had something to do with it, sure, but his intelligence, his background, the ability to speak multiple languages, and his sense of grace and style, probably shouldn't be left off the list. Of course, Fiver would say, with his southern grace and humility, his partners in crime, the ones who helped him… they were the reason for his success. He took care of them and they took care of him. Some of his English friends told him they should call him, the Scarlett Pimpernel, after the famous story. His companions and accomplices, were a tight knit family of thieves.

Fiver stretched his arm muscles behind his back and twisted side to side to limber up.

A few of the older women, sitting above and behind him in the upper deck, shifted sitting positions in their deck chairs, trying to get a better look.

Fiver Dean, at one time, one of the most athletic and coordinated students at the University of Cambridge, formerly a well trained, fighting machine with the French Foreign Legion Special Forces, and at the top of his present profession, as one of the most notorious art thieves in the world… finished stretching his back and his shoulders… took three steps toward the pool… and BAM!

What happened next, was the start of the most remarkable chain of events, accurately and duly reported in the Interpol Historical Records, and the day Fiver Dean would never forget… for the rest of his life.

Trying to slide his foot into one of his imported, Grecian sandals, being somewhat new and stiff, it caught on his heel and tripped him, causing him to fall, and then slip… and then bounce, his head off a poolside table… before tumbling into the water butt first… throwing his plastic glass of Bloody Marys, into the startled group of world traveling soccer moms, who milliseconds before, had wanted to have his baby.

It was such a hilarious, comedy scene of a 'good looking, cool guy' ... furniture, arms, legs and alcohol flying through the air, and then crashing in the water, even Special Agent, Aurora Aria Romana, had to stop and step back from the balcony rail. It was impossible for her to laugh and breathe... and hold the binoculars steady... all at the same time.

She managed to control her laughter for a second, and looked back over the balcony railing, through the binoculars, just in time to see the dark image of Fiver Dean, sinking to the bottom of the pool.

After she hurriedly got the high powered, lenses, refocused on the pool below, she noticed Fiver Dean's dark image in the water... wasn't moving.

Chapter Two
**'When A Black Browed Albatross
Tries To Kill You'**

A black-browed mollymawk, gliding in the sky above, flapped it's wings downward to lower its altitude and circled the tiny figures below. If the bird had the gift of thought, it was probably wondering what all those ant size creatures were doing, flailing around in the funny looking pond below. Black-brow Albatrosses live up to seventy years old, and this particular bird was five years past that, with failing eyesight, age-worn wings and a bad back from long flights on Saturday nights.

Besides the Albatross, there were different types of birds, flying high above the hotel roof. They were diving for food, thrown by hotel guests from their balconies. It was fun to watch the birds dive at incredible speeds, to retrieve the food thrown into the air. Large birds would snatch whatever was offered in midair, and then catch an updraft to take them high into the sky. The hotel had signs posted in each room, instructing the guests to NOT feed the birds, but the message was normally ignored.

The old, single albatross, had to bide his time because of the competition for the food. He was much slower than the other birds and the timing had to be perfect for him. He circled the sky, intently watching for any movement along the hotel balconies. He would be ready when his time came.

Bianca Pericoloso, startled as Fiver Dean fell into the pool, choked on the Greyhound cocktail she was sipping. Holding her head back and gasping for air, she burst out laughing. Echoes of giggles and laughter from the crowd, who had witnessed Fiver's ungraceful entrance into the water, reverberated around the pool.

It seems Bianca had been laughing, ever since she had been introduced to Fiver. He had become one of her best contacts in France, because of his uncanny ability to acquire certain collectables, that her specialized clients desired. His sense of humor and personality, made him fun to do business with. And now, this unflappable and GQ looking man's fall, had looked like a clip from 'The Best of The Benny Hill Show', flopping into the water amongst the other swimmers.

She stood up, eager to see how her charming business associate, would react after making a fool of himself. Her sides were still shaking from laughter.

In her balcony room, Agent Aurora Aria Romana, had stopped her giggling. She watched the pool water through the binoculars.

The water in the pool swirled as the crowd of people waited for Fiver to resurface. The sound of laughter had subsided to a hum of anticipation of what the good-looking gentleman would do, and what he would say, after coming back up from his Three Stooges fall.

Nothing happened.
There was no movement from the blurry image on the bottom of the pool.
The sloshing, white-capped pool water, violently awakened by Fiver, was starting to calm, an unwitting partner to the building suspense.
Bianca took a step closer to the pool. She unconsciously put her hand to her throat.

Aurora Romana did not hear her partner re-enter the room with the take out food he had gone for. She eased her body further over the flat top balcony rail, and turned the knob to refocus the binoculars toward her view of the pool and the dark shape in the water.
"OK, Romana, here's your food," said Felipe Forbeian, Detective Grade of the Polizia di Stato. He set two bags on a small table by the sliding glass door. The short, stocky man had been Aurora's liaison with the Italian police for almost 1 month.
"Anything happening with our boy?"
Aurora waved him off impatiently. "Shuuuus," she said, " somethings going on here." She continued to stare through the high powered lenses.
"Aww, he's ok," said an old woman on vacation from West Virginia, USA. Mildred Worthmore, heiress to the Worthmore Mining Company fortune, was sitting in an electric wheelchair, by the upper deck table, with a large

drink in front of her. She didn't seem to notice or care, she was the only one still laughing at the clumsy fall of the cute boy, she had put on her glasses to get a better look at. She had a quarter inch of sun block, on her face, with brief areas of bare skin, showing thick painted-on eyelashes, arched below a deep wrinkled brow. It was such an outlandish look, it was hard for people not to stare at the old lady, especially the kids, who thought the old woman was a clown. She had not been born into wealth. Her father had made his fortune when Mildred was in her early twenties. She knew what it was like to work for a living. She also knew how it was to be rich. She was old and senile and an alcoholic. She didn't give a damn about anything.

"I've fallen harder than that off the toilet," the old woman said, slowly maneuvering a huge glass of Jack and Coke to her mouth, with shaking hands, and after touching her lips to the rim, taking several huge sips of the south's finest.

A noticeably embarrassed younger woman and man were sitting beside her and seemed to be her caretakers. The woman reached out and put her hand on the elderly lady's arm. She said quickly, "Granny, please. Your voice is too loud, people are looking ."

"Screw em and the mule they rode in on," the old woman said, putting the drink down and waving her arms indignantly. "this is a great show!"

The younger man turned to his wife beside the old woman. "Unbelievable, we should have left her in West Virginia", he said, "the doctor warned us traveling might make her worse".

Mildred Worthmore's granddaughter's husband, Bruce Killoy had not complained at first, when the couple was asked to accompany the old woman on a trip to visit her mother's birthplace, somewhere in Italy. He thought the trip would kill the old woman. With his wife's name securely in Mildred Worthmore's will, he really didn't care if she made the return trip with them in a First Class airplane seat, or down in a box in the cargo area.

The old woman slammed her empty glass into Bruce's chest. "Here", she said," Get them to fill this back up…chump." She tilted her head back and laughed at her rhyme. She didn't like Bruce and didn't try to hide it. She turned back to the pool area.

Bianca Pericoloso knelt down by the pool. She thought she saw Fiver move. He was deep, near the pool drain.

She called out, "Fiver, Fiver… quit playing. Come up from there!"

The young, blond, teenage lifeguard, sitting on the chair perched above the pool, had been watching the scene unfold. She stood up, slowly, and took off her loose cover-up, revealing a bright orange bikini. She was not quick to respond to men this age. She had been taken in before by these middle-age perverts who would fake a problem, just to get a free feel when she came to their aid. She was going to be sure there was really a problem before entering the water. She watched the figure at the pool bottom intently.

The old albatross flying overhead, caught an updraft and climbed several hundred feet before starting back toward earth. Several guests threw Italian baloney off the balcony and the food fell quickly toward the beach. Before the older bird could react, there was a flurry of wings, and the morsels were retrieved by diving younger birds. The old bird continued to ride the currents and bide his time.

Bianca put a hand into the water and made sweeping splashes, to get Fiver's attention.

"Fiver!" she demanded, " Get up here now!"

A few of the men, standing around the pool, had

seen what happened, realized there was stress in the young woman's voice and moved, as if to assist her. They obviously had read the chapter in the Single Man's Handbook, which describes the strategy of offering themselves as a hero to any beautiful woman in need. This strategy has been used down through the generations for young men to put themselves in a position to help a damsel in distress, with the reward being a possible overnight relationship, with any damsel inclined to give that type of reward to the ambitious 'single man'. It was always worth a try, in their one cell mind, even though there has been no scientific proof or data, that confirmed the 'Be A Hero' ploy has ever worked, or would work in the future, for the 'single man' to actually attain any type of such reward. None of the men, in their zeal, realized Bianca Pericoloso was so far out of their league, they never had a chance.

The figure at the bottom of the pool suddenly moved upward as if shot from a cannon.

Fiver Dean ejected himself high out of the water and took a huge breath of air. He moved with grace and fluidity in the water. He looked like a trained dolphin at Sea World.

"TA DA!" he shouted as he landed, head held high, in deep, but shallower water, waving his hands above his head in the best Broadway, dramatic flair he could muster. It was the perfect response to such a slap-stick entry into the pool.

He pushed his dark hair from his face and turned in circles, acknowledging the round of applause from the people poolside.

Mildred Worthmore, the old woman at the upper deck bar area, laughed at the sigh of relief from the crowd and said, "See, I knew that faker would be all right. Send him up here, he can change my diaper." The bartender, standing there, turned away so no one would see him laughing.

"Granny! Please!" the young woman beside her exclaimed, but tried to hide a smile. After all, she WAS Mildred Worthmore's granddaughter.

"I'm going outside", said Bruce, her husband, visibly embarrassed. He was a surly, unpleasant sort of fellow. He got up and left.

Bianca Pericoloso stood up and put her hands on her hips. All the predatory males who had headed her way, disappointingly turned back to their solitary lives on the sidelines. Bianca had not even noticed their existence. She waved her hand at Fiver angrily, and returned to her lounge chair. Removing a towel from her beach bag, she reached down to rearranged the contents inside, making sure the transmitter's microphone was still connected to the velcro faster inside the bag. She spoke underneath her breath, but loud enough for the receiver to pick up the sound of her voice. "I'll never get anything out of him if he kills himself," she said into the microphone.

Aurora Romana chuckled as her informant's voice, crackled over the speaker. She glanced at the video camera beside her to make sure a clear feed was coming through the monitor. She turned back to the athletic man, clowning around below, walking in chest high water toward the pool steps, and waving to the cheering crowd. This guy won't last a day in prison, she thought. Someone will throw him through a window for fun.

The old black-browed albatross, glided through the air above, turning his head side to side. His wings were straight and still as he watched the crowd below him. The prime birds of his species normally weigh around ten pounds. Lack of food and extreme age, had reduced the weight of this bird somewhat, and caused him to be more alert than usual for the possibility of a free and easy meal. Could be a chance for some ripe pickings below, if he was lucky. The bird kept circling in the sky.

Detective Felipe Forbeian, of the Polizia di Stato, approached Aurora with a questioning look. "What's going on?" he said, "Any word or sign of who his accomplices are? That's why we're here. Right? We could have clapped cuffs on him two days ago. What's up?"

"No," the young woman said thoughtfully, without looking at Forbeian, "We've got him cold. If anybody can get it out of him, it's Bianca. But, she knows better than to rush him. He's got some kind of antenna when something doesn't feel right. I've chased this guy for two years. I know him. She can't spook him now. If we can get the other's names, fine, if not, he is still going down today". Aurora turned toward Felipe and looked straight into his eyes. She continued, "He's not someone to fool with."

She set the binoculars down and started to stand up, chuckling while remembering Fiver's fall. She had gotten so involved in watching the craziness below, she had forgotten the red, plastic, 32 oz. cup full of ice and diet soda she had previously prepared and started to drink before the commotion, and had left on the balcony rail. As she turned toward Felipe, her elbow knocked the cup off into the wind and the Italian landscape below.

"Oh my God," she whispered, as she desperately reached out to try and catch it.

In the past, while in the sky, the old albatross had been occasionally lucky when a tourist would throw food off their balcony, and he would beat the other birds to it. Now, the bird, even with it's failing eyesight, was the first to see the red snack, falling toward earth, and saw an opportunity to get the jump on the other birds.

He turned a wing downward and started his power dive.

If there had been no wind that day, the cup and it's contents would have fallen straight down into an area only inhabited by plants, flowers and a huge water fountain. No problem.

As it was, there were higher than usual air currents that day, flowing in and above the coast.

Catching the glass, the ice and the drink... a particular high gust of wind, moved the cup's descent, directly toward the pool area.

Seeing the people and children playing below, Aurora instinctively started shouting, "Look out below, look out, look out!"

Detective Felipe rushed to the railing in time to see the red 32 oz. plastic, cup with the soda and ice intact, knuckleball downward.

"Uh-oh, that doesn't look good," he said.

Fiver, hearing the warning from above, turned his face toward the source of the shouting.

The red 32 oz. plastic cup, with all of it's contents still in it, flew through the air with remarkable accuracy, hitting Fiver Dean, the world's foremost and sought after, art thief, square in his Hollywood, handsome face.

BAM!

Oh, that hurt.

Fiver cowered and winced from the stinging varieties of pain, in his head and face, as everything suddenly hit him. He dropped his head and squinted through hesitate eyelids upward, and saw a slim woman, holding what appeared to be binoculars, looking down at him. Even at that distance he could see her short Auburn hair, and the concerned look on her face.

So, I didn't die in an oven, he thought. They're trying to kill me with plastic.

He stumbled in the water and felt a wave of dizziness. He was about to pass out. That plastic cup had some force to it. He looked up.

That split moment was when the black browed albatross, being extremely hungry, and hurtling down in a power dive for the red, 32 oz. plastic cup, thinking it was a bit parcel of hotel food… unfortunately misjudged his descent by distance and angle, due to light and shadow, contrast and windspeed… because the old bird was ninety percent blind… and dived straight into Fiver Dean's face with a violent impact that was terrifying to see and hear. It was with enough force to knock the wading man back into the water with a crash.

The laughter and cheering, coming from the crowd before, suddenly turned into hysterical cries and screams, as bright red, blood and feathers appeared on the top of the waves of water, where the bystander's children, wives and husbands, had just been enjoying the cooling water.

The teenage lifeguard, who had been easing back into her chair, without hesitation, arched her back and dived into the water after the sinking man.

Felipe Forbeian, Detective Grade of the Polizia di Stato, looked at the flurry below, took a deep hit on his favorite French Vanilla nicotine juice, and somberly said, "Wow, now, that… REALLY doesn't look good."

"Come on,' said Interpol Special Agent, Aurora Aria Romana, grabbing her bag and hurriedly patting her side, to check the gun attached there, "We've got to get down there now! Let's Go!"

The two officers ran from the room and toward the elevator.

# Chapter Three
## 'Don't Look At The Naked Lifeguard'

Bianca Pericoloso screamed, and every male, who had turned away in defeat and mediocrity, in their response to her seconds before, now charged the pool and jumped in after the teenage lifeguard, and the sinking man. It was a total circus of bedlam, with people and a wild bird, flopping around in the water.

Fiver Dean was knocked back into the water and thought he heard, as he was falling, something about somebody should throw the drowning man a life preserver. It was vague. But, that's what he thought he heard.

He was knocked silly. Dazed. Easing in and out of blackness. Life preserver. Yea. Poor man needs help.

He kept reaching outward. Arms didn't seem to work. Breath knocked out of him. He kept trying push out his arms, reaching for the flotation device that never came.

Throw the damn life preserver already... let's go, somebody, I'm really dying here.

Desperately holding his breath and trying to keep consciousness, Fiver finally saw the life preservers, somebody had thrown, coming toward him. He thought, thank God, and reached upward, and grabbed a preserver tightly in each hand... hold on now, Great! Safe! He waited to float back to the surface.

The young female, lifeguard, swimming to Fiver's rescue, screamed and kneed Fiver in the chin, knocking him deeper into the pool and oblivion. She swam back furiously to the surface, yelling obscenities. She was covering her chest with one arm as she jumped from the pool, and ran to her dressing room, more mortified about her nakedness than the drowning of the pervert she had almost decapitated.

Fiver sank to the bottom of the pool with the lifeguard's orange bikini top, still clasped in his unconscious hands.

Reaching down, more interested in vying for the attention from Bianca Pericoloso, than saving any drowning American, several of the poolside cowboys, swimming behind the lifeguard, had pulled Fiver up and out of the pool and laid him on the ground by the pool ladder. They walked around his body, all with great heroics, slapping each other on the back and shouting hurrahs for each other's effort.

Several of the soccer Moms, seeing Fiver lying there, seemingly unconscious, moved quickly to his side to perform CPR and mouth to mouth, if provided an opportunity. They had no shame in pushing their way in front of the other women, who were slow in recognizing the possibilities with the handsome man, prone on the ground.

Bianca, rushed over, waved the other women off, and knelt down beside Fiver, yelling for somebody to get a doctor.

Blood was oozing from his nose, trickling down into his ear. His black hair, dripping water, was pushed back against his head. His eyes were opened. Unfocused. But opened. His breath came in shallow gasps.

Bianca, for a second, thought of how peaceful he looked, almost childlike, cradled in her lap. She almost felt guilty about helping to put him in jail. Better him than me though, she thought. Lover. She bent down to kiss his cheek.

"Talk about crazy stuff happening, wow... they've called a doctor for you. That bird almost took your head off.", she said excitedly in his ear. She started rubbing his chest.

She pulled a handful of feathers sticking from Fiver's nose and threw them aside.

Fiver started to stir and slowly come around.

The old albatross was paddling around in the warm water of the pool, the empty, red 32 oz. plastic cup was in his beak, seemingly not to worse for wear. At the last moment, the old bird had realized his navigational error and tried to pull up out of the dive. Only semi-successful, the bird had managed to prevent full speed contact into the human's face, but the glancing blow from the bird, had resulted in Fiver's nose being pushed halfway up the bird's ass. The old bird jumped out of the pool, waddled to the edge, and flapped into the air before any type of attempted capture could be made. The empty, red 32 oz. plastic glass was dangling from the bird's beak, as he disappeared into the sunlit sky.

Fiver lay on the ground, looking up into the concerned faces of Bianca and the crowd gathered around him.

A few wispy, white clouds drifted in the blue sky above him.

His eyes turned toward the balcony, where it all started.

The woman, with the short, auburn hair, and binoculars, was gone.

Fiver started to struggle to regain his feet. His legs weren't working properly. Bianca tried to help him up and she slung his arm around her shoulders. Being small, she was having problems getting the heavier man up to her side.

A young woman with a yellow beret, covering her head and dressed in a light blue coverup, stepped from the crowd and took Fiver's other hand. She draped Fiver's arm around her neck, taking weight away from Bianca.

Fiver groggily turned to the women to express his thanks. He had taken a tremendous smack on the head.

The Good Samaritan woman, who had taken the initiative to assist them, waved her hand as a 'you're welcome' sign, and helped Bianca walk Fiver to the nearest lounge chair.

A medical person on the hotel staff, pushed his way through the crowd, and knelt beside Fiver. "Tell me what happened sir," he said, "are you in any pain?" He opened a bag he had set on a table beside Fiver.

"You wouldn't believe me…Doc," slurred Fiver, "I saw the inside of a bird from the inside…". He drifted with the blackness, trying to take over his body.

Aurora stepped out from the crowd, stopped and confronted the two women and Fiver Dean. Detective Forbian and two other uniformed officers, were standing behind the Interpol agent.

"I'm afraid," she said, 'this is as far as Mr. Dean goes." She held out a badge with her credentials. "My name is Special Agent Aurora Ramona, with Interpol and this is Detective Forbian with the Polizia di Stato."

The woman, in the yellow beret and blue coverup, who had helped Bianca with Fiver, stepped back, and faded into the many faces of the crowd of people surrounding them.

Agent Ramona motioned to the police personnel, standing behind her, to move in around Fiver.

Bianca said to Aurora, "Hey, I think he really is hurt…?"

"Thank you, Officer," Fiver said to Aurora, moving his head side to side and dropping it in her direction. He started to drift toward total unconsciousness and darkness and said," I want that bird arrested and charged with attempted murder." His head rolled back, as he blacked out.

The two women stood over Fiver Dean, as he laid back onto the lounge chair, locking their eyes together as his head touched a rolled up towel.

"I might have gotten it all, if this hadn't happened?" Bianca Pericoloso said to the agent, "The deal was for tonight. He hasn't left my side. We'll never know who else is involved, now."

Aurora hesitated in cuffing the man, who was now breathing deep and regularly into the arm of the lounge chair,

"He was having a good time," continued Bianca,"he didn't seem like he was in a hurry to go anywhere. The paintings are in his room. I saw them wrapped up, inside the clothes closet. The meeting was set for tonight for the money exchange."

Fiver sounded like he might start snoring at any minute.

'Too bad," the Interpol officer said, standing up to face the other woman, "We had to take him down now. I wouldn't trust him if he was in a full body cast, being fed through a tube. This guy is as slick as they come. Its been two years, but I finally got him. I can't risk letting him slip away."

"I hope he's going to be ok," Bianca said, wistfully stroking Fiver's hair back from his brow.

The unconscious man seem to smile at her touch.

She continued, "Did you get everything you needed?"

"Yes, video and audio in the can. Evidence tight enough to send our boy here away for some time. Ole Fiver Dean has stolen his last art piece and will be headed to a French, concrete gallery full of people just like him. He sure put on a show his last few hours as a free man, didn't he? That bird was something. YouTube would love that one."

A higher ranking member of the hotel medical staff, appeared and examined Fiver. After a few minutes, he looked at Aurora and said, " He'll be ok I think. A busted nose, and looks like a possible concussion. We'll need to take him to the hospital to fully check him out. I've given him a shot for pain and swelling."

"Fine," she said, "we'll send uniformed officers with you."

"Too bad," Bianca said gently, as she moved aside to let the attendants get closer to Fiver " I hope you'll not be to mad at me, handsome."

She took her hand from Fiver's face.

Aurora looked at her. "Any other info he might have given you? Something we might not have gotten on the wire? Anything about who else he was working with?" she said, with a tinge of hope in her voice.

"No," said Bianca, "I couldn't get any more out of him. We played cat and mouse most of the time. I don't think he suspected me…but, you never know about Fiver. I've never met or seen anybody who worked in his crew. It was always just him and me."

Aurora looked at the beautiful, Italian art fence, she had used in the sting against Fiver Dean. Bianca Pericoloso had been busted in a stolen art sting in Rome in the fall of last year. The Polizia di Stato had asked for Interpol's assistance in the sting, and after confronting Bianca with the evidence that would have put her in prison, she wanted a deal. Her lawyers presented the powers that were, a plea deal where Bianca would get immunity if she could offer up the most sought after art thief in Europe, the one the "Gendarmerie nationale", or French police, called 'L'Art Fantôme' or 'The Art Ghost'.

There had been an added asterisk and star, in Special Agent Romano's personnel file, the day she was chosen to be the lead investigator, in the investigation of 'L'Art Fantôme'. Once a mysterious criminal, now, Aurora thought, we know all about you. There had been no name, no description, no clue, on the art thief, who had been plaguing rich art collectors and museums all over Western Europe. She had been on the case for two years without much, if any progress…and then she got the call about Bianca, a person inside the inner circle, who had actually fenced Fiver Dean's stolen artwork in the past. Aurora Romano had been almost giddy to finally be closing in on her prey.

The Interpol agent looked down at the man beside her. It didn't bother her to send him to jail. He was a crook. He was a good looking crook, but still a crook.

The young woman, in blue, who had helped Bianca move Fiver after the bird catastrophe, pulled her yellow beret down on her face and eased out from under the shadows of the overhead deck area. She had been closely watching the law enforcement officers now surrounding Fiver Dean. She moved outside to the hotel entrance, moved through the crowd. and abruptly vanished, into the stream of hotel guests, entering the foyer.

Two Medical Personnel rolled Fiver Dean onto a stretcher, strapped him in and started to wheel him from the pool area and outside to an awaiting ambulance.

Aurora stopped them and handcuffed Fiver's wrist to the stretcher railing.

"That will hold him," she said.

The men rolled the stretcher through the lobby and placed Fiver into the back of the ambulance. They locked the stretcher into place and while one EMT stayed to checked the vitals of Fiver, the other EMT closed the backdoor. He stood waiting for the uniformed officers, who were to guard Fiver Dean on the trip to the hospital. The officers had walked to the other side of the parking area to retrieve some equipment, and then started back toward the ambulance.

That was the plan.

It didn't happened that way.

If it had, Fiver Dean would be in jail and Bruce Killoy would still be alive.

# Chapter Four
## 'Fiver Dean Escapes'

The medical attendant, standing by the ambulance door, told authorities later, all he saw was a woman's face in the side mirror when the vehicle sped off without warning. He thought she might be wearing a yellow hat, maybe a blue or green, some type of shirt. He said he couldn't make out her features too well. It happened too fast.

The police, realizing what was happening, when the ambulance squealed out, pulled their weapons and fired as the emergency vehicle turn off the drive, and disappeared around the corner of the hotel.

Bruce Killoy had been standing on the sidewalk, behind the entrance wall in front of the exit door. He was smoking a Salem, just outside the border line limit of a No Smoking sign, and fuming because of the amount of attention his wife was showing to the old lady. His wife and grand-mother-in-law, had left the pool area and were searching for him to get ready to go to supper. The two females came through the handicapped side door which exited right behind Bruce. He was busy watching the police and the ambulance activities in the entrance drive and did not notice or hear, Mildred Worthmore, drive up behind him in the electric wheelchair. Stopping beside Bruce, she wound her arm up and violently slapped him on the back, while she yelled, "Come on Chump, Get ME A Drink!"

The sudden force on his back from Mildred's blow, plus the sudden yell in his ear, pushed, startled and caused Bruce Killoy to jump off the sidewalk, from behind the wall, and into the open drive, right behind and a split second after the ambulance rounded the corner and disappeared.

The police stopped firing, after three rounds had been discharged from their weapons, toward the rear of the moving ambulance.

One round hit the bumper, ricocheted off and embedded into the hotel sign. The other two rounds ended up in Bruce Killoy. One round hit him in the knee, the other straight through his heart.

Mildred sat, and her granddaughter stood, on the sidewalk…in shock. Frozen. Neither of them moved.

Silence.

'Oops…", said Mildred.

Special Agent, Aurora Aria Romana, had left after the medical personnel took Fiver away, and had gone upstairs to his hotel room. She was desperate for evidence and clues about Fiver's alleged partner or partners, but mainly wanted to retrieve the million dollars worth of stolen art Fiver was trying to fence. Bianca had confirmed the paintings were in Fiver's room. Her snitch had seen them. Afterwards her investigation would be finished. Maybe time for a holiday.

The sense of relief and success for her, were replaced by a burning anger, after she heard gunshots from the hotel entrance and learned of Fiver's escape. She immediately got on the radio to Polizia di Stato to organize road blocks and to coordinate their assistance. All hell was breaking loose. Suspect escaped! Citizen killed. OMG! There were going to be some heads rolling and butts chewed. The icing on the cake was…she did not find any of the stolen art where Bianca said the paintings would be.

The EMT, in the back of the stolen ambulance, was being thrown side to side, banging his head on a number of pieces of equipment as they sped over potholes and various speed bumps. The ambulance suddenly squealed to a stop in the middle of the road. The EMT was moaning and sprawled out on the floor. He lifted his head up far enough to see the door, leading to the front cab of the ambulance, slide open. A young woman with striking features, was turned around in the driver's seat, facing him. She motioned with a small gun in her hand, toward the back door. The frightened man nodded, and scrambled out the back. He fell prone to the road and kept his head down until the ambulance sped off.

Fiver Dean, drifting in and out of consciousness, after being tossed around in the ambulance, held his head up, to see his arms strapped down and a wrist in a handcuff, attached to the stretcher.

He looked through the sliding cab door.

The young woman was driving furiously around corners, and darting down any side street that appeared. She managed to glance at him occasionally through the rear view mirror.

Driving in intense silence, she said nothing for a minute. She looked at him angrily.

"You've had a busy day, " the young woman finally said, turning her head sideways to him, "You know Bianca, that bitch, betrayed you... set you up, and the law was there to catch the whole ride in High Def and living color. I've had eyes on you the whole time, you idiot. Got the paintings from your room, too boot. Now, that was a trick, I tell you, with all those Federals hanging around. What were you thinking? That witch of a woman? Remember our meeting tonight, probably not? How's the head? "

The barrage of words and emotions from the young woman came like a southern tornado. Fiver had trouble keeping up with the rapid fire tongue lashing, he was getting from the raging female.

He laid his head back on the stretcher and managed a pained laugh. The bird had knocked the senses out him.

Concussion maybe? He had forgotten all about the paintings, and the meeting, and the driver, and everything else that had happened before his encounter with that stupid bird.

"So, I've gotten you to thank for being slammed around in this four wheel hospital' he said, with reluctant recognition, but an appreciative tone.

"Yes, you do," the driver said,'at least you're not in the pokey. I may kill you later, but that remains to be seen…"

"Oh, ok, you win," said Fiver Dean.

"Thanks, now find me a doctor, my nose and head are killing me. Damn bird." He put his free hand to his head.

She finally grinned at her accomplice and seemed to enjoy Fiver's discomfort. There was an Italian doctor, she had used before, who didn't ask too many questions, and lived in a villa close by. That would be the place to get Fiver back on his feet and then out of the country.

The young woman thought about payback for a rat with long blonde, hair. Revenge would be sweet with the satisfaction, she thought.

She tapped the leather holster of the gun beside her leg, with a long, manicured fingernail.

If you want to stay healthy, Joyce 'George' Dean, thought… Don't mess with my family.

## The End

Thank you for purchasing Fredonia Bound

## Look For
**SannaBlue Baker's Music**
# Spotify!

**Facebook – SannaBlue**
**Twitter – @sannabluetn**
**Instagram - sannbluetn**

# Get To Know The Author

Gary 'SannaBlue' Baker has entertained people with stories and music, since his childhood growing up as a preacher's kid, in the shadows of the Great Smokey Mountains in Tennessee. Gary shares his home at the Sanctuary on the Hill in Fredonia, Tennessee, with his friend, Bella and lives life doing what he loves... writing, photography and making music.

Bella